PUFFIN BOOKS

THE WORST SOCCER TEAM EVER

Never was there a more unlikely band than the Greenhill Intermediate School 'C' team. What a bunch of sporting also-rans! They were all shapes and sizes, from the captain, 'Tom-tit' Colman, to 'Griller' Spinks, goal keeper simply because he filled the goal so completely. Then there were the girls of the team: Lavender Gibson (Lav for short, because she wanted to be a radical feminist plumber when she grew up), and the pink and delicate Maggie Smith — she even dressed in pink on the field. As for Ms Hennessy . . . Cinderella's pumpkin would have made a better coach. She even called practice 'rehearsal'!

The Worst Soccer Team Ever is an hilarious tale. Our humble narrator, Tom Colman, has total recall – which means he's remembered word-for-word everything everyone said. Except for the bits he had to make up. You've heard of poetic licence? Well, this is poetic lying.

BY THE SAME AUTHOR

My Summer of the Lions
Shooting Through

THE **WORST** SOCCER TEAM EVER

WILLIAM TAYLOR

PUFFIN BOOKS

Puffin Books
Penguin Books Australia Ltd
487 Maroondah Highway, PO Box 257
Ringwood, Victoria 3134, Australia
Penguin Books Ltd
Harmondsworth, Middlesex, England
Viking Penguin, A Division of Penguin Books USA Inc.
375 Hudson Street, New York, New York 10014, USA
Penguin Books Canada Limited
2801 John Street, Markham, Ontario, Canada L3R 1B4
Penguin Books (N.Z.) Ltd
182-190 Wairau Road, Auckland 10, New Zealand

First published in 1987 by Reed Methuen Publishers Ltd, New Zealand
This Puffin edition published by Penguin Books Australia Ltd 1989

3 5 7 9 10 8 6 4

Copyright © William Taylor, 1987

Produced by Viking O'Neil
56 Claremont Street, South Yarra, Victoria 3141, Australia
A Division of Penguin Books Australia Ltd

Text design by William Hung
Typeset in Plantin by Meredith Typesetters, Melbourne
Printed in Australia by The Book Printer, Maryborough

National Library of Australia
Cataloguing-in-Publication data

Taylor, William.
The Worst Soccer Team Ever.

ISBN 0 14 034002 5.

I. Title.

NZ823'.2

CONTENTS

CHAPTER ONE

IN WHICH WE LEARN A TRULY VALUABLE LESSON

'We're gonna do ya,' said one.

'We're gonna waste ya,' said another. 'Can't wait,' and he grinned evilly.

'Won't know what hit ya,' said a third.

'I would think we'll just have to see about that.' I tried to sound very confident. I have found it's the only way to deal with people like this. They may look big, they may talk big, they may even smell big but, like soldiers, anywhere, going into battle, they usually sound more confident than they feel.

'Can't wait,' breathed the second one again. He turned to the other two. 'Let's go warm up. Not that there's much need for these poofs. Look at 'em.' They all laughed, and then took off.

'We'll just wait and see,' I called after them, loudly. 'Apes!' I whispered. I find the only way with this sort of person is never to buy an argument. Mind you, you'd think a church team would have a bit more Christian charity. You just never can tell these days. St Joseph's. Where, indeed, was their simple milk of human kindness and good sportsmanship? Could it be that it was hidden beneath their tough and rough outsides? Well, there was a little lesson to be taught to this lot and very soon. This was likely to be the most radical, creative and total game of soccer they'd know this season. The end result would surely see them shocked and gasping. Defeat, not that they knew it yet, was staring them in the face, and all brought about by the simple application of intelligence to what, after all, was no more than a game.

Time to look for my team and try to spot Ms Hennessey, our charming coach, who was supposed to have remembered the jerseys. Just the sight of Griller, our goal keeper, was enough to lighten my load and make me feel heaps better.

'Where's me jersey?' he yelled. 'Come on, Colman. Where the hell's me jersey?'

'It's okay Grill. Don't you worry. Ms Hennessey'll get them here.' Knowing our dear Ms Hennessey I was none too sure of that. After all, she had promised them to us a week ago and we still hadn't seen them.

'Ask me, she don't know what time of day it is,' said Griller.

Privately, I was forced to agree. Still, as they say, we don't all run to the same sort of clock and it was hardly Ms Hennessey's fault she'd got us to coach in the first place. It had been fate that made her cough at the wrong time.

'Yeah, well, I want me jersey,' said Griller.

What is a captain to do? Griller Spinks is our second-string, and quite an important weapon. Griller Spinks, real name Dwayne. Griller is short for Gorilla, and with one truly excellent reason: he looks like one. Griller, our goalie.

Griller Spinks is enormous and has great long arms. Big! He's very big with a body that just about three-quarter fills the goal. What his body doesn't cover his arms do. Anti-social, is Griller. He does everything he shouldn't. A great law unto himself, as the saying goes. Swears, blackmails, steals, smokes, fights, tortures, bullies, drinks, and I hear he does all these things away from school as well. My very good friend and close associate, Lavender Gibson, reckons that Griller could even supply pot if you needed it. Her friend Maggie told her and someone else had told Maggie. It was my great hope that by involving Griller Spinks in the sporting world at a responsible level it might be possible to do something for him. In the meantime, need I add, he could do something for us by stopping the ball getting into our goal.

'Come on, Tom-tit, Sweetie,' yelled Lavender, my very dear friend. 'Where's the jerseys, then?'

Sometimes I wish that Lav would keep the pet names of our private life to herself. 'They'll be here, Lav. Don't you worry.' Close friend and companion she might be, but she sure has one loud voice. I must ask her not to call her team captain Sweetie in public.

'Yeah, Sweetie,' yelled Griller. 'Where's me flamin' jersey?'

'Let's get this over and done with, Tommy,' said Lavender. 'You know it's my shopping morning. The Presbyterian Ladies have got this lovely load of new stuff in and I want to get there before everyone else gets their paws on it. I want a new coat and you're coming with me.'

We waited for ages. Still no Ms Hennessey. The rest of the team were impatient and Griller said he was going to leave. At the last minute she arrived. I wished she hadn't bothered. I could have died. The little old white van with all its stickers chugged up the street. No one could miss it because it was surrounded by a cloud of blue exhaust smoke and sounded like ten chainsaws.

It didn't stop in the car park with all the other cars. Oh, no. Ms Hennessey ploughed straight for us across all the playing fields, dodging players and spectators and ignoring all the very wild signals to stop. She pulled up behind the goal Griller would soon defend, and brushed aside the arm-waving ref and several parents of the other team who tried to have her on.

'Got here, pets. The good Lord knows how. We've been half across the country looking for this place, haven't we Mitch? Now get those jerseys for these kids and don't let Persil out of the car. Quick, pets, we're late.'

She was telling us? Mitch was Ms Hennessey's close friend and companion. Persil was her cat and was just as savage and untamed as Griller Spinks. Ms Hennessey was also just about the strangest looking coach these grounds had ever seen. She wore a tartan blanket with a hole in the middle for her head to poke through. In places it came down to the ground and in other places just below her waist around which she had tied a dressing gown cord.

Lav's eyes glowed with approval. 'She looks a dream, doesn't she, Tommy?'

'You got two minutes, lady, to get this lot on the field and that wreck off the grounds,' said the ref.

'Knickers to you,' said Ms Hennessey, which I thought was as good a way as any of putting this little official in his place. She and Mitch dragged a canvas sack from the back of the van.

'Can't you read the council sign, lady? No vehicles or animals on these fields. It says so. Teachers! All the same, you lot.'

'Come on, pets. Come and get them. Mitch says they're all the same size.'

They were. Outsize!

'Massive,' said Lavender, pulling one over her head. 'Couldn't have done better myself, Ms Hennessey. Can I keep mine when this is all over?'

'Thought you'd like them, pet,' said Ms Hennessey.

Massive? Massively and truly dreadful. A major disaster. Once upon a time these jerseys had been red. Now they were pink. To really rub it in they were old, very old rugby jerseys. The size was bad enough. The colour was bad enough. The wrong sport was bad enough. But there was still worse. Every one of them was covered in holes. I don't know whether it was moths or old age or some poor Mum going wild with the bleach. These might well be fashion garments if found at the Presbyterian Ladies, but as my old Mum, Mrs Colman, always says, 'There's a time and a place, Tom.'

The roars of laughter started quite little. It is my experience that hysteria often does start little. Then they grew. The only ones not laughing were us and poor Ms Hennessey. Even her Mitch laughed, until she looked at him in that way that Lav often does at me.

'Hey, you guys! Someone shoot your jerseys, eh?' yelled one of the other team. That really got them going. It takes very little for some people to just about wet their pants.

'Not gonna wear this thing,' said Griller.

'Now, Dwayne. It's just your size and looks lovely,' said Ms Hennessey.

'It's okay, Ms Hennessey,' I said quickly. 'Griller's in goal and he doesn't have to. He should have a different one anyway. Seeing as you didn't get him one he can just wear his own.' Griller was in luck.

The ref came over. 'You get this load of pinkos on the field now, or the other lot get it by default.'

We tucked our jerseys into whatever we could and took the field. This was it! The Big Time had arrived.

There was me, Tom Colman, centre-forward and captain of Greenhill Intermediate School Soccer Team C. My fellow forwards were Lavender and Wilson with Maggie and Brian outside them. At right and left half were Gordon and Nick, with Boggy in the centre. Peter and Paula, our team twins, were the backs and good ole Griller was in goal.

A fine and misty rain fell, but it didn't dampen our spirits. It just dampened us. And now to our minute of truth. Our shining hour and a bit, if you count half time. The jerseys mattered no longer. The laughs and jeers of our opponents faded as had done the sun before the rain came. The hassles and agony of even getting here were forgotten. There would be no laughing after this. No way. Any laughing would be on the other side of their faces, after we'd shown them the way to go. Way to go!

My pink team. The creation of my mind. So proud I thought I'd burst. St Joseph's, eat yer heart out!

'It's take-ya-to-the-cleaners time, kid,' said my opposite number. 'Take ya to the cleaners where those jerseys sure haven't been.' Chuckle, chuckle, chuckle. 'Can't wait for this.'

Well, he didn't have to. Not for long, anyway.

32–0.

32–0!!!

We lost our second-string weapon thirty seconds after we started. Goodbye Griller. The one who was going to take us to the cleaners kicked the ball right at poor old Grill. Caught him, it did, right in the guts. Griller booted the ball across two other fields and then took off and caught the St Joseph's centre-forward and did him on the spot. It took all the spectators, me, the ref,

Ms Hennessey, Mitch and Lavender to drag old Griller off.

The ref was, as one might expect of a man of his rudeness, quite unreasonable. 'I'd have the little sod for assault if it were my kid. Get off! Go on. Get off!' Then he yelled at Ms Hennessey. 'Get . . . him . . . off!!!'

Ms Hennessey didn't have to bother. Griller took himself off and treated the ref and our opponents to one of his fine performances of spoken and sign language. A master of the sign language; I've often thought Griller would have been happier and a bigger success in life if he'd been born deaf.

'You lot can play with ten men.' The ref continued to be unreasonable.

'Ten persons, you mean,' said Lavender.

'Look, girlie . . .'

'We only got ten, anyway,' I said. 'Paula can go in goal.' Poor Paula. Poor us.

The only time the ball came our way was when I got to kick off. In the whole game there was only me, and Griller at the beginning, who got to feel that lump of leather.

It is easy, readers, to criticise our play. Yet, in all honesty, I must admit our tactics were perfect. We moved forward as planned; lightly, easily, elegantly and with no waste of movement. Just as we had studied, hour after hour, watching *Match of the Day* on telly. What was right for the big boys would be right for us. It made sense. Perfect sense. A kick here and a volley there. So simple and so direct.

It should have worked. Sheer intelligence must overcome brute force. It didn't.

St Joseph's were devils. They were everywhere. In and around us and destroying, crushing our carefully designed plans. Wham, wham, wham. Bang. Wham, wham, wham, and bash it in at poor old Paula.

'Stop it!' I yelled. 'Stop them, Paula.'

'How?' An anguished cry from her heart.

'Come on St Joey's. Give it to them!' yelled a parent. 'That's it, Mick. Drive it home. Show 'em how it's done. Beat the little runt, Mickey. Do him! Good on yer, man.'

They were animals of the lowest order and their kids were no better. 'Told yer we'd waste ya,' said one of them, lazily. 'And now we done it.' He wasn't puffing, not at all. 'It's beautiful.'

Was this, I asked myself, a Christian team?

Just before half-time Ms Hennessey joined the game. Not that she meant to. Even the St Joseph's team looked startled when she screamed, 'Persil! Mitch, I told you to keep that damned window closed.'

Black as the night, her cat, Persil, streaked across the field with Ms Hennessey right behind him. Across the next field and then another one. Under the club-house right over on the other side.

'Looks like you've lost ya best player,' smiled the captain of the other side. 'Bad luck.'

'Black cats are a traditional sign of good luck, actually,' I told him.

'Reckon no one told that cat,' he said.

'I knew I shouldn't've got up this morning,' said the ref, and blew his whistle for half-time.

Lav, Boggy and Mitch went to help Ms Hennessey but it was okay. She had caught Persil and held him tight to her with a lower bit of her blanket. 'Naughty boy. You naughty boy.' She spoke to Mitch. 'Now put him in the van and keep him there.'

'I told you to get that thing off the grounds,' said the ref.

'He's not on your precious grounds. I'm holding him. Can't you see?' said Ms Hennessey. 'And now he's going back to his van.'

'Was the van I meant,' said the ref.

She ignored him, as any lady would. 'Now, pets. Time for a wee pep talk. I think we might be holding them.' The score was 14–0 at half-time. 'That was a lovely move of yours, Tom, the last time you kicked off,' she said.

'Yeah. Until he fell flat on his face,' said Lavender.

'Well, pets. Only the start of the season. Very first game.'

First and last. Not again, I thought.

'You're doing remarkably well, pets,' said Ms Hennessey. 'That nice red-head boy in the green. Beautiful little mover, and great pace, I think they call it.'

'He's on the other side, Ms Hennessey,' said Bog.

'Goodness. Is he?'

'Have you ever seen a soccer game before, Ms Hennessey?' Boggy asked her.

'I'm not too sure, pet. Maybe not. Not really my cuppa, as they say. Still' – she sure was bright – 'I'm absolutely positive you're holding them. Come on, now. Smile. Mitch, get us the barley sugar from the van and don't let Persil out.'

The second half was worse than the first. Their coach told them to be kind to us. I heard him. This did not please their three supporters one little bit. 'Let them get stuck in. What's he think this is? A game?' – and other kindly expressions of support. Their animal team did as they were told, and not by their coach either.

Toe to toe and toe to chest. Chest to toe and head. Would it never end? Dear God, please end it. Toe to toe and plop, into our goal again.

32–0.

'Good effort, pets,' said Ms Hennessey. 'I've heard worse scores.'

'Not in soccer you haven't,' said Mitch.

CHAPTER TWO

IN WHICH WE GO BACK
TO THE GROUNDWORK

'How'd it go, kid?' asked Dad. 'All the plotting and planning and sitting in front of that damn video pay off, eh?'

It beats me how some people can never resist getting to the heart of a matter. 'Well, er . . .' I say, very slowly.

'Give 'em a walloping, then?'

One thing about my Dad. Once onto a good thing and he knows never to let it go. Should've been a cop, I reckon.

'We did not enter this competition, Father, in order to wallop people,' I say with considerable dignity. 'We . . . er . . . made a reasonable start. In the circumstances, I think we could certainly say we made a reasonable start. One or two things to iron out. That's all.'

'What was the score?' Dad asked. 'You did win?'

'Sort of not exactly.' It's important to keep your cool with people of this character. I've learned that from Lav.

'What d'you mean, not exactly? Seems to me that not exactly winning sounds a helluva lot like losing.

Wouldn't you say? Sort of like, well, going down the gurgler? Come on. You can tell me. What was the score?'

I told him. He whistled. 'Wow! Sure some gurgle.' He smiled a truly cruel smile. 'I did offer to help. Remember? You can't say I didn't. Sure wasn't very nice for me to be spurned, turned down for the sake of a video.' He smiled some more of his cruel smile and looked for all the world like one of the St Joseph's team. 'As they say, you can only get better. Better luck next time, kid.'

'There isn't going to be a next time, Father.' I call him 'father' when I wish to show deep displeasure. I think it annoys him greatly. Not that he's ever said so. 'There's not going to be no next time. Not never.'

He looked at me and the grin got worse. He's a sadist in his spare time, my father. 'Reckon there is, Tom old sport. Well, almost sport.'

'Me and Lavender decided on the way home,' I said. 'She said we shouldn't waste our youth on misspent effort.'

'Did she?'

'I agree. It was stupid to . . .'

He cut in, sharp as a knife and ten times as cutting. 'Stop feeling sorry for yourself, Tom. All your bright idea in the first place, and after all the fuss you've caused you're going to see it through. Don't care if the score was 132–0. You've disturbed the lives of a dozen or more people; kids in the team, their parents who've spent a fortune buying boots, all the people at school. What about this Miss Hennessey of yours?'

'What about her?'

'Think of her. You are her team.'

'She wouldn't even know what sport we were playing. She's not the sort of teacher who is truly into sport,' I said.

'Well, you're not giving up. No matter what Lavender says. It's back to the drawing-board, I reckon. You've got a week to do something in.'

'Fortnight. We got a bye next Saturday.'

'Sounds as if it's just as well,' said Dad. 'You're going to need every hour God sends. Now, then, let's get inside. Your mother and sister will be dying to hear all about it. Pity you wouldn't let us all come. Could've done with a chuckle or two this week.' He had one now.

I loathed and despised everything this individual stood for. As you may all clearly see, I am blessed with a parent of great insensitivity.

He was right. Dead right. They couldn't wait to hear. Not like any normal family who take no interest at all in their kids' personal and painful disasters. My lot never failed to take a big, big interest in all my ideas.

'For goodness sake, Tommy. Not another of your hare-brained schemes,' Mum had said back then in those happy days before the disaster. 'It still seems like only yesterday when you were going to be a marathon runner and go to the Olympics.' She had smiled a shark-like smile. 'I'll never forget it.'

Well, neither would I. I could still hear the ambulance siren and the guy yelling to the cop that how the hell was he to know? All the other runners had passed by here a good half-hour ago, and he thought the little old lady was yelling at someone to stop me because her bag had been nicked. That's the only reason he ran into me on his bike.

'It's just that I contend . . .' I began.

'Here he goes again,' said Sue Colman, my sister. She's four years older than me and a true pain. 'I've heard it all before, Mum. Like the time he contended your umbrella was a parachute and took off from the garage roof. Stop him, I beg you.'

'I remember, dear. He wrecked all my lovely old-fashioned roses in their first flowering.'

No one at all worried about how they'd wrecked me. I had given up using that excellent saying 'up yours' some time ago.

'Let him finish,' said Dad.

'It's beautiful. So simple and involves next to no work at all. None of you'd have to help. Not this time,' I said.

'Pass your plate, dear. I'll give you the rest of the custard. Build up your footballing strength. Footballers need their strength,' said Mum.

Which showed her level of sensitivity. She knew I couldn't stand custard. Who can? 'All I was going to say before being rudely interrupted by each and every one of you, was that if you apply intelligence and intellect to any situation you gotta come out on top. Even in soccer.'

'That's nice, dear,' said Mum.

'I think you should be good enough to let our World Cup soccer squad in on your secret,' said Dad. 'Reckon they'd be more than grateful. Anyway, why this sudden interest in sport? Not like you, Tom. Except for your very short career as a marathon runner . . .'

'A well-rounded man needs well-rounded interests,' I said. 'I contend that sport should be one of those interests, and healthy minds live in healthy bodies.' I looked, pointedly I thought, at that part of my father's body around the waist that was very certainly well-rounded.

'Listen to him. You're still a little boy, Tommy,' said Sue.

An icy ignore is the only way to treat many people. Sue was one of the many. Besides, she was wrong. I was nearly thirteen. Very long, and sometimes painful discussions with my companion, Lavender, had told me, if I needed this telling, that not only did I have the right attitudes to life, but also the right equipment for a man to get through it. Lavender assured me that it was only a matter of a very short time before, as they say, everything came together. It did seem, though, in the privacy of my bedroom, that certain bits of some significance had better get a move on. To be absolutely truthful, which I must try to be, I do admit that at nearly thirteen I am still a rather small hunk. Lavender always says, 'Size isn't everything. It's what you do with what you've got that counts, Tommy.' Fine for her to say; she's twice my size, and this presents another problem for me to surmount on life's way.

I spoke to my sister. It's not something I enjoy doing. 'I intend getting into soccer this year. And let me tell you, if we had rugby I'd be getting into that.'

'What as? The ball?' said Sue.

'I've put my name down for it. So's Boggy and so's Lavender.'

'Do they allow girls in the team, dear?' Mum asked.

'They haven't so far, but Lav reckons they're about to change their thinking.'

'I reckon they will, too,' said Sue. 'After all, she'd be a darn sight more use in the team than you and Bogdan put together. Lavender Gibson's sure one well-rounded man. And Mrs Lupescu's not going to let Bogdan play. Not ever. He'd never have the time, and he'd hurt his hands.'

'That's enough, Sue,' said Mum. 'I think it's all a lovely idea, dear. If that's what you want, you go for it. And it does sound quite normal for a change.' She had to spoil things.

'We thought marathon running was normal, too,' said Dad. 'Remember?'

'Hmm. Yes. Still.' She brightened. 'It certainly beats spray-painting, doesn't it?'

Would they let me forget nothing? I shall not continue to relate this discussion. It is too recent, too painful in more ways than I care to mention. It had been my dear friend Lavender Gibson's idea to spray anti-apartheid slogans on the public toilets. I never could see what she called the symbolism of it all. I've never known a public toilet that was a racist symbol. The only thing we learned from it all was how to spell racism.

It is one thing to say you are going to play sport. It is quite another thing to take on the establishment and actually get in a team.

It wasn't that our school was not big in sport. It sure was. We had teams for just about everything. They call it 'character building'. But no one, it seemed, was very much interested in building our particular characters. It's a great truth that schools really only take an interest in those who can play sport well. Those whom the good Lord has blessed, sort of. Those of us not built like born winners only ever got to toddle round a field or a court on sports afternoons when nothing got organised and half the kids snuck off, followed by half the teachers going to look for them. Those who were left scragged each other, which I suppose is a kind of sport.

To those who have got, it shall be given. So it says in the Bible, and I agree. It all means that the big-time Saturday sport got sewn up by those who've got what it takes. In other words, they got it given to them in heaps while the rest of us missed out.

Seventy-five of us kids had turned up for the meeting in room 15. Seventy-four boys and Lavender.

'There'll be two school teams this year. Got most of it sorted out from the lists that went round the classes last week. Most of those who played last year are playing again this year. We won't need too many try-outs.'

As I said, 'sewn up'.

'Why can't we have more teams, Mr Crow?' I asked. 'There's hundreds of us here.'

'Interest fades, lad, and don't interrupt me. Just enough here for two teams. Those who don't get in a team'll have a go as emergencies. Only two of us coaching this year. Me and Mr White. What's that girl doing here? Netball meeting's in Room 12, dearie.'

'I'm here for soccer, Mr Crow,' said Lavender.

'Made a mistake, dearie. Don't have girls' soccer,' he chuckled. 'Netball meeting in Room 12.'

'I want to play soccer,' said Lavender.

'Girls don't play soccer,' said Mr Crow.

'This one does,' said Lavender. 'Well, to be truthful, Mr Crow, this one is going to.'

'Over my dead body,' said Mr Crow, quite politely.

'If that's the way you want it, Mr Crow,' said Lavender. 'I'll be ringing the Human Rights Commission tomorrow morning.'

'Out! Out! Out! No one speaks to me like that. Not in twelve years.'

The fat was in the fire, as they say, so I helped it along. 'Maybe you could tell us, Mr Crow, under what rule or law of Association Football girls aren't allowed to play?' I made sure I was very polite. These older people lose their marbles over such little things.

'Out! Out! Out! We can do without your sort here! Been here twelve years and we can do without your sort.'

17

'Perhaps there is a . . .' began Boggy. That's as far as he got.

'Out! Out! Out!'

'I was only trying to help him,' said Boggy when the three of us were out.

'You would,' said Lavender. 'Anyway, it didn't get us anywhere.'

'It got us out here,' said Boggy, reasonably.

'We may be out,' I said. 'But not down. We shall leave no stone unturned, and I'm going to see Mr Harvey. Maybe he'll do something.' Mr Harvey was our school principal and a greatly respected older gentleman who quite often didn't know the time of day, a bit like Ms Hennessey.

'You've got quite a problem, John.'

'Tom,' I said.

'Yes, Tom. You're our marathon runner, aren't you? Thought that might've given you enough of a taste of sport to last a lifetime. Room 16?'

He seemed pleased to have almost put a face to a name. 'Sort of,' I said.

'Sort of in Room 16?'

'Next door. Room 15.'

'Well, John, it's like this. I don't interfere with the sports programme. It doesn't pay me to. It's delegated, I'm pleased to say.'

'Someone told me you stopped us having rugby,' I said.

'Not quite right, Don. Rugby's a wonderful game, a real game.' He sounded sad. 'It was a democratic decision, see?'

I didn't see. 'Oh?'

'Sign of the times, Don. The younger staff, really. Pressure. Couldn't be seen to be supporting apartheid. Radical action they called it. I called it pressure. Now

18

I can place you, Don. Yes. The man who does sign-writing on public property. It's Tom, isn't it?'

'Yes, Mr Harvey,' I said. Quite a nice old guy, really. Near retiring, I think, in his late forties and quite elderly. They say as old folks get older they lose memory cells from their brains at an awful fast rate. Mr Harvey had clearly lost a very great number.

'You're the feller who's always asking questions. Now I've got it. Had a sister here two or three years ago. Lovely, quiet, bright girl.'

Which proves my point. Poor old soul, it must be hard. Still, it wasn't the time to put him right.

'You know, Mr Crow has put many years into our sports programme, and far be it from me to interfere. It's his pigeon, as the saying has it. Never been too happy since we did away with rugby.' He sighed again. 'You've got to sort it out with him, Don. That's it. Fair enough?'

'I have a feeling that won't be too easy, Mr Harvey.'

'Give it a go, lad. Give it a go. Boy of your character. Your mother's some sort of lawyer. Right?'

It's truly amazing how the adult mind works. What did my Mum's job have to do with anything? 'Part-time, she is,' I said.

'Wish I'd had the sense to take up law,' said Mr Harvey. 'Be driving a Mercedes by now, I would.'

Clearly he hadn't spotted our car, one of the bigger embarrassments in our suburb. Still, if it made him happy. 'Yes, Mr Harvey.'

'Well, Don. Give it a go. See Mr Crow.' Mr Harvey chuckled at the sound of his own wit. 'Give it a go. See Mr Crow,' he repeated. 'And don't you hesitate to drop by this office any time you've got any little problems need airing. Door's always open.' A most kindly man, with good intentions.

19

See Mr Crow. No go. Summed it up. No coach. No field. No shirts. No ball. No hope. 'Besides you've left it too late, lad. Meeting was last week. Sorted it out then.'

'I know, Mr Crow. I was there.'

'Well then, lad. Your name'll be down somewhere for something.'

'I don't think so. I had to leave early, Mr Crow.'

'You're too small, anyway,' he said.

'I really don't think, Mr Crow, sir, that size has very much to do with soccer playing ability,' I said. 'I am light on my feet, and marathon running has made me right quick at dodging things.'

'Tell that to the marines,' he said.

'I don't think the marines play much soccer, Mr Crow.' I drew myself up to my full height and spoke with cold politeness.

'Out! Out! Out!'

It often puzzles me that even with all my great politeness I still get these quite negative responses from those who should know better. Still, as they say, that's life, that's the kicks.

Lavender, Bog and me – back to Mr Harvey. His door was closed but we knocked and waited.

'A deputation, I see, Don?'

'Tom.'

'How's your mother, then?' asked Mr Harvey.

'Mrs Colman's fine,' I said. Maybe the old boy wanted some free law work. 'Mr Harvey, we have come to see you to ask if there would be any objection to us organising a third school soccer team of mixed sex and ability, and finding our own coach and jerseys and playing fields? And there's any number of persons who would like to have a go and we are quite responsible and would do everything we can to uphold the truly good name of Greenhill and all that goes with it and in no way would we be a drain on the meagre resources of this great school.' That was a right good one. He was always going on at us about our meagre resources and if we lost library books we couldn't buy paint for art. 'We would even meet all expenses for the team out of our own pockets, sir. Mr Harvey, sir.' Lay it on thick and nice. They love it this way. Gives your older type of person a real power buzz.

'Yes,' said Mr Harvey.

'Yes, what?' said Lavender. I had told her to be polite.

'Yes, there would be plenty of objection. That was John's question,' said Mr Harvey.

'Why?' asked Bog.

'I've had a chat with Mr Crow,' said Mr Harvey.

'The old boy network at work,' said Lavender. 'Sexist politics at work again.'

I kicked her. 'Shut up, Lavender.'

'No, Mr Harvey. I will not be shut up,' said Lavender.

'I wasn't trying to shut you up, Lavender,' said Mr Harvey. I noticed he never made a mistake with *her* name.

'You see, Mr Harvey,' said Lavender, 'I don't really blame Mr Crow.'

'I'm really glad of that, Lavender. As far as I can see he's not guilty of anything. Other than doing his job, that is.'

Having made an opening, Lavender did her best to get right in and stuff it all up. 'It's not really Mr Crow's fault, sir, that ultimately he is a victim of his own racist and sexist conditioning. It's the system.'

'We didn't come here to discuss all this, Lav,' I said.

'You mightn't've, but I did,' said Lav. 'It's what it always boils down to. Your good old politics of sex and race.'

'No it doesn't,' said Boggy. 'All we want is a chance to play soccer in a school team. If we can't do that, then all we want is a chance to set up our own team through the school.'

'Well put, Bogdan,' said Mr Harvey.

'Even in adversity you men always stick together,' said Lav.

Mr Harvey did his humble best to steer us clear of sexist political waters. 'I can't see your parents being very happy about your playing, Bogdan. What about those hands of yours?'

'You don't play soccer with your hands, Mr Harvey,' said Bog. 'Besides, I'd wear woolly gloves.'

'How about it, Mr Harvey?' said Lav. She used a bit of her own sexual politics and fixed him with a number one stare from her gorgeous violet-blue eyes. It just melts my heart when she tries this on me. Women. They sure have a way with them.

Mr Harvey did a melt-down. How could he do otherwise? 'Shall we say a provisional yes,' he said.

'What does that mean?' asked Boggy.

'It means just that,' said Mr Harvey. 'You do all that Don here says you will and I can't imagine any of us objecting. Are you sure you've got a team, Don?'

'Just about a hundred, sir, turned up for Mr Crow's meeting. There'll be a lot of them want to play for us.'

'That remains to be seen,' said Mr Harvey, looking at the three of us in turn.

'We're going to put a notice on the noticeboard, sir,' said Lavender. 'We've done it out already. Then we'll see.'

'Just one thing,' said Mr Harvey. 'You must have a coach, a person responsible for you who is on the staff.'

'Sir,' I said. 'We were going to do it ourselves. We don't need a teacher coach in charge of us.'

'You heard me, Don,' said Mr Harvey.

'That's done for us,' said Boggy.

'Never,' said Lav. 'Can we come to the next staff meeting, Mr Harvey, and do a PPP? We could make a heartfelt appeal.'

All schools have odd things. This was one of ours. Dear Mr Harvey did not blink. Well, he wouldn't. PPP was his little baby. His Pupil Participation Programme. He gave the first ten minutes of every staff meeting to the kids. Anyone who wanted to could come along and have a moan, a groan or ask a question. As you may well expect, next to no one ever turned up. So much for democracy. Lavender was the biggest pupil user of the opportunity. Lav, and her one woman friend, Maggie, often used his ten minutes for their campaign to clean up the school library of sexist literature. Nothing much ever happened about their complaints so now Lav and Maggie burned Biggles books privately. My Mum, Mrs Colman, says she admires their ends but can't approve of their means. She reckons a free society is built on tolerance. Lav says that's all right for my Mum, who is older. She, Lav, says she has never thought much of free societies anyway, and there's always people who have to be told what's best for them.

I am clearly blessed to have the love of such a strong woman, but I told her to keep her mouth shut and her hands to herself if she really insisted on coming along to PPP with the staff of our school. They are an oldish lot and have never got used to her radical feminist ways. In the time we've been at this school Lav has put the backs up of all of them. While this might say something about their backs, I wasn't going to take a risk. I told Bog to shut her up if necessary and let me do the talking. The talking or the pleading or the greasing. I am able to sound so much more humble than Lavender. I think my size has something to do with it.

Who am I not to grasp at every opportunity or port in a storm? We turned up to PPP at dear Mr Harvey's next staff meeting and to take the bull by the horns.

'*The Concise Oxford Dictionary* of our language describes sport, among other things, as "pastime, game; outdoor pastime, e.g. hunting, fishing, racing, especially making good bag or basket when shooting". It goes on to say, ladies and gentlemen, that a good sport is a "person who regards life as a game in which opponents must be allowed fair play; person ready to play a bold game . . ."'

'Get to the point, Don,' said Mr Harvey. He was always so ready to encourage us, his pupils.

'You should try teaching the little . . .' I didn't hear the next word. 'He never does get to the point.'

'What Tom means,' Lavender began but Boggy, bless him, shut her up.

'What I mean is, I appeal to you today, you teachers of this great school,' laugh, laugh, laugh inside, but grease on . . . 'to come up with, for us, a person who regards life as a game, as the immortal *Oxford Concise Dictionary* says it is, in which opponents must be allowed fair play. Don't, I beg you, shoot us down, as the OCD says, before we have sunk that good bag and basket.' Somewhat puzzling, all this, but bound to impress them. The only thing teachers like better than a bit of original research is going to the pub on Friday afternoons. I've looked in the window of the lounge bar of the Greenhill Tavern when they've been there.

24

You wouldn't believe it. A truly disgusting display. I reached the climax of my appeal and announced good and loud, 'We need a coach.'

'Cinderella used a pumpkin,' I heard a smart one say. I have a feeling it was Mr Crow's hatchetman, Mr White. He was younger than a lot of them, and that sort are usually smart at us kids' expense.

'Fair hearing, staff. Fair hearing,' said Mr Harvey. 'Come on, Tom.'

He got it right, bless him. I went back to my notes.

' "Good bag and basket." We need a coach for our soccer team which Mr Harvey in his great and kindly wisdom . . .'

Cough. Cough. Cough. Surprising how many of them seemed to have colds. Probably a result of always having their desks next to the heaters and then going out into the cold night air.

'. . . has said we can have for the upcoming inter-school Saturday morning competition, if we can discover one of your generous number willing and able to keep an eye on us from time to time and not often . . .'

'To coach you,' said Mr Harvey, a slightly sharp tone in his voice. 'Supervise you.'

'A hope in hell there,' said Mr Crow, but I noticed Mr Harvey didn't seem to hear him.

'So, today, dear staff, we appeal to you for a mentor; that's one who is an experienced and trusted adviser and comes from the Greek . . .'

'Save us from any more of the dictionary, John. Now then, you've had your say and our time is precious. Lot more to get through today,' said Mr Harvey.

'I can only thank you, Mr Principal, for your great personal sympathy and generosity in allowing us to present our case for a coaching person for our soccer team, and ask the one amongst you who will accept this honour to now step forward and . . .'

It was at this moment that Ms Hennessey coughed very loudly and we got our coach. She always tried to say, the dear thing, that all she was doing was clearing her throat. But that was enough. And I do think, in all truth, it was more than that. My words, my message, as Lavender would call it, had truly got through to her. Ms Hennessey was it.

Mr Harvey was very quick at accepting Ms Hennessey's kindly offer. They can move quick when they need to, these older ones. 'My dear Miss Hennessey, this is the first time you've spoken up in a staff meeting since you became one of our number. Thank you. Thank you. John's team are all yours to do with what you will. Quite a load off Mr Crow's plate. Off mine as well.' Chuckle, chuckle.

Ms Hennessey opened her mouth as if to speak but then she coughed again. She was it all right.

'Don, Lavender, Bogdan, you've scored quite a victory indeed,' said Mr Harvey. 'Not easy in these days to persuade a member of staff to give up their Saturday mornings and most nights of the week as well, for a game of sport. You make sure you thank Miss Hennessey very nicely. A very kind offer, Miss Hennessey. Thank you.'

'Yes, Mr Harvey,' Ms Hennessey now had her vocal chords under control. 'It's . . . it's . . . just that,' she looked at the three of us in that way we have come to know and admire so well. 'My pleasure to be of any assistance . . . I think.' She smiled a little smile and left it at that.

Obviously the rest of the staff were just as delighted with our success. There were many smiles, and one or two sitting next to our coach, Ms Hennessey, were clapping her on the back in congratulation. She had started to cough again which was a pity, spoiling her enjoyment of what must have been a wonderful moment for her.

CHAPTER THREE

IN WHICH WE TRY TO FORGET
ABOUT 32–0

'If you look at it one way,' said Lavender, '32–0 is not entirely a disastrous start.'

'You could have fooled me,' I said. 'What way's that?'

It was pouring with rain. We sat under Lavender's large, yellow golf umbrella on the steps outside the branch library. Our favourite place to be together. Only half the umbrella had cloth covering it. That wasn't the side being held over me.

'I think,' she said, 'we must look at it as a starting point. A sort of launching pad from which things can go forth and only get better.'

'Couldn't get much worse, could they?'

We had done the Presbyterian Ladies Op Shop and Lavender had put a down-payment on her very first fur coat. Once upon a time it had been a sort of mud-coloured rabbit, but now it was little more than just skin with surprising tufts of rabbit fur here and there. 'I do realise animal skins are much, much better on animals. Still, you must admit, it's a bit late to help these ones now,' said Lavender.

'You're right, dear. I don't think any self-respecting bunny would be asking for them back,' said a Presbyterian lady. 'That'll be ten dollars.'

Lav knocked her down to eight but still didn't have enough to buy the coat outright.

'We don't cater for lay-by, dear. Still, as you're such a good customer we'll keep it for you till next week. Goodness knows what your Mummy'll say about this one.'

'My first fur coat and still only thirteen. Not that I approve,' breathed Lavender.

'Of course not, dear. Still, roll on the first mink, eh?' said the Presbyterian lady.

'It's only partly a fur coat,' I said. 'You mustn't always be letting your principles stand in the way of your life, Lav.' I think I made her feel better. I tried on the perfect flashers' coat. Truly lovely. An old, faded grey, and it came all the way down to my ankles.

'Three dollars, dear,' said the Presbyterian lady. 'Mind you, I could swear you've already got one like it.'

'I always say you can't have too much of a good thing. Years of wear in this,' I said.

'You can surely grow into it, dear. Three dollars?'

'Two dollars.' You've got to be tough with these women.

'Done,' said the Presbyterian lady.

They sure could get business-like, these church shopkeepers. These ladies could get blood out of a stone. Sometimes, if they were not busy, they'd give us a cup of tea and we'd have a chat. I think it was their public relations exercise for good customers. Not today. They had half our suburb in there sheltering from the rain.

'We'll have lunch outside the branch library before we do the Sallies' garage sale,' said Lav. 'I just feel it's time to think summer wardrobe. Summer madness!' she yelled and one or two people looked at us. 'I can't wait.'

29

'You're going to have to wait, Lav,' I said. 'It's still the beginning of winter.'

Lunch was a little bit miserable. It was cold. A gale was blowing and even the rain seemed more wet than usual. We were the only people on the steps of the library and it was still an hour till the Sallies opened. However, you can never be too downhearted when you're with the one you love.

'Down but not out,' said Lav. 'Cheer up.'

'You sound like my father.'

'As I've sometimes said, that man speaks a lot of sense,' said Lav.

'I reckon we should give the soccer away. Cut our losses. We're going to be one big laughing-stock.'

'Speak for yourself. I've never been a laughing-stock in my life,' said Lavender. 'It's back to the drawing-board, man. Not going to let a stupid game of soccer beat us. Steel yourself.'

'Down and not out. Back to the drawing-board. Every cloud has a golden lining, eh Lav?'

'Silver lining. And, dear Tommy, I have found it's no use trying to deal with you when you're in one of these black moods of yours. I think you must be Irish. Either that or it's because you're a man.' She snorted. I think some rain had got up her nose. 'In my experience that's the trouble with men. Never had to face adversity.'

'Neither have you, Lav.'

'If only you knew,' Lav sighed.

'I do.'

Lavender Gibson, apart from being my very dear friend, was also just about almost my twin. Only thirty-seven hours and nine minutes separated us. She was the older one, naturally. As she says, it makes quite a difference. Lavender's Mum, Mrs Poppy Gibson, and mine, Mrs Colman, had even shared the same room in the hospital where we were born. As Lavender says, undoubtedly they had also shared their very first hopes and fears for us, their children. She even reckoned we had probably drunk the milk from each other's mothers from the overflow Lav says they keep in the fridge for hungry babies. 'The nurses use it for their cups of tea, too. Saves a bundle on the cow stuff, and much more nutritious.' She had put me off any sort of milk for a year.

Lavender Gibson, daughter of Mrs Poppy Gibson. Sister of Carlos Gibson, well-known hunk, eighteen years of age. Tall, blond and handsome, and looking like a telly commercial for pimple stuff after the stuff has done its work. A man to be looked up to, Carlos. Mind you, I have to look up to most men anyway. Lavender said Carlos was a racist pig, treated all women as sex objects and had very dirty bathroom habits. Lavender said that she was of the opinion that Carlos would never outgrow his adolescence. Who am I to disagree with Lavender?

For all that, dear readers, I would sell my soul and body to whoever wants it, if in return I could come back to this world of ours as a Carlos Gibson look-alike. It is my experience that it is to the Carlos Gibsons that this old world gives up its treasures in great heaps.

There was no Mr Poppy Gibson. There had been two: one for Carlos and one for Lavender. According to Lavender and to my Mum and to Boggy's Mum, Mrs Lupescu, all the danger signs were out that Mr Poppy Gibson Number Three was just around the corner. This did not please Lavender Gibson, who said that no self-respecting woman needed a man. This did not please Carlos Gibson, who considered himself man enough for any house. Quite rightly, bless him.

31

Mrs Poppy Gibson was one of our suburb's better known business persons. She owned the Poppy G. Boutique and Accessory Bar. Lavender and me were only allowed in if we went straight through to the back room. 'I love you both dearly, but no one in their right mind could call you walking advertisements for any shop.'

This was okay by Lav because her mother's business was truly embarrassing to her, trading as it did on the stereotypes your less than desirable men have of women. For all that, Lav and Mrs Poppy Gibson were the very best of friends. 'We're more like sisters really,' Lav would say. 'And you can't hold it against poor Poppy that she's a product of the highly sexist fifties.' She called her mother Poppy to everyone else, and Mummy to her face.

What a woman! Mrs Poppy Gibson was the great party-giver of our suburb. These days she was hot on what she called Ethnic parties, and a night at her house was not a success unless you could spot a Samoan, a Tongan, a Vietnamese, a Kampuchean and at least one American Black, in addition to what our green and pleasant land normally produces. My Dad called it tokenism and Lav agreed. My Mum said it was okay by her, and Mrs Poppy Gibson could invite who she liked, and she just hoped she wouldn't go back to the olden days when she sorted people out for her parties by the jobs they did. My Mum always got invited as 'my friend, the lawyer.' It was far nicer these days, my Mum said, to just baby-sit Lavender. She didn't have to baby-sit Carlos. He was too old. Besides, he'd been going to the parties for years because he was a social asset and good at mixing drinks. A very great drink-mixer, Carlos.

Mrs Poppy Gibson's new boyfriend, and soon to be

stepfather of Carlos and Lavender, was her latest ethnic person. He had taken some finding. Your American Blacks don't grow on trees in our suburb. Eugene, of Pocatello, Idaho, was sure some American Black. There was two metres of him. Two metres exact and he was out here playing for one or two seasons for the Johnson Potato Crisp Suburbs United National League basketball team. When he wasn't basketballing he was a Phys Ed major at a North American university studying Phys Ed, Sport-stress Counselling and Shopping Mall Retailing as well as Medieval Poetry. It was through Shopping Mall Retailing, rather than basketballing, that he had met the love of his life, Mrs Poppy Gibson.

Mrs Poppy Gibson sure is no dwarf, but she did look like one when you saw them together. In fact, it looked as if Eugene was twice her height. Still, who am I to say what makes a perfect pair? They sure seemed to be in love. I pointed out to Lav there was some danger of her mother being tripped over by Eugene. The poor guy wouldn't be able to see her. Also, if it was a very dark night Mrs Poppy Gibson would have very great trouble locating Eugene. Lavender gave me a lecture on sexism and racism after that lot. I was surprised because Lav was dead set against them getting married. First, she didn't want a stepfather and second, she reckoned the age difference was too big. Eugene was twenty-one and Mrs Poppy Gibson was slightly elderly.

I reckon Carlos' reasons were far more animal. Quite simply, he couldn't face the competition.

Eugene didn't have much conversation. I had tried many times on a number of interesting things about the state of life in the good old US of A. I am vitally interested in the way our northern hemisphere brothers are getting on and how they live and do things. No go with Eugene. About all he ever said was, 'Hi there, you all,' or 'Here's a stick of gum, kid. Use it.' Still, more than likely he and Mrs Poppy Gibson made up for it when they were alone.

The Salvation Army garage sale was a true wash-out. A storm-water drain overflowed and most of their good stuff floated off down the street. 'I thought we were here to get your summer wardrobe,' I said to Lav after she had bought three pairs of long-johns for a song.

'This rain tells me we've still got winter to work through,' she said. 'First things first. Come on. Let's go home. I'll make us some pancakes. Then we'll get down to some real planning about the team.'

It was all I needed to hear. The memories came flooding back. Still, the pancakes sounded right okay. Soccer? My brilliant career was dead.

Mrs Poppy Gibson and Eugene were taking in a movie down town and only Carlos was home. 'Good game, Lav?' he asked.

'Don't call me that.'

'You win?'

'There's far more to life than winning. To some of us winning is an ugly word. To win means you have to clobber some other poor person.'

'You lost?'

'Sort of,' I said. Here he was, too, sounding just like Dad.

'Get hammered, eh?' Carlos grinned.

'If you must know, the score was 32–0. Now then, shall we leave it at that?' said Lavender.

Carlos laughed. He laughed so much he choked, and Lav had to belt him on the back. Still he couldn't stop, so she belted him harder. She seemed to be enjoying herself.

Lavender, Lavender, you are so right, I thought. He is a slob. One vast adolescent slob. Down the plug hole with any regard I ever had for him.

He got himself part under control. 'Say it again. Please, Lav, say it again,' he kind of half choked.

'If it makes you so happy, and also if you promise to choke again,' said Lavender. '32–0.'

He sniggered and sniggered and then dragged out a pack of cigarettes. Slob Carlos.

'Don't you smoke in here,' said his sister. 'My friend and I don't choose to be endangered by your second-hand fumes. It's as bad for our health as it is for yours, and I'm going to tell Mum.'

'Up yours,' said Carlos, and settled back, still chuckling. 'You need a hand?'

'I'm perfectly capable of making pancakes by myself, thank you,' said Lavender with what I thought was great dignity and style.

'Stuff your pancakes. I meant with your team?' Carlos blew a foul cloud of smoke right at Lavender.

This was no time for false pride. If she wasn't going to reply, I was. 'Yeah,' I said. 'You gonna help us?'

'Over yours, kid. Me?' he smiled, real evil. 'I'm into other sports you kids wouldn't of heard of. But I got an idea.'

'Poor idea! It must be awful lonely in there,' said Lavender beating the hell out of her pancake mix. The butter in the frying pan was burning more smoke than Carlos and it sure was getting hard to breathe.

Carlos ignored her and leaned back in his chair. 'That friend of yours, Maggie. She in your team?'

'All of our team are our friends,' lied Lavender. She sure was wrong. Griller was no one's.

'Maggie. You know the one?'

35

'I might,' said Lavender.

'D'you want me to help or not? Please yourself.'
Carlos lit another cigarette from the butt of his first.

'I couldn't care less.' Lavender poured batter into
the smoking fat.

'Well, they've got this granny flat out the back of
their place,' said Carlos.

'I know, dummy. They used to have a granny to go
in it,' said Lavender.

'Yeah, well, she croaked or they dumped her in a
home. Something like that,' said Carlos.

'You've got it all wrong, as usual,' said Lavender.
'Grandma Smith became incontinent and wet her pants.
Maggie says, and I agree with her, that it all became
too much for her mother to cope with because, after
all, she had her own life to lead too. If she was forever
changing Granny Smith she wouldn't ever have a chance
to lead it. So they put her in a home for her own good.'

'God, you sure go on,' said Carlos.

Privately I had to agree. The care of the very, very
elderly was quite interesting and a problem all of us
would have to face one day. But it wasn't helping with
our team, and I said so.

'Shut up, Tom-tit. I'm getting to it,' said Carlos,
quite nicely. 'I'm only trying to help you. You sure
do need some help.'

I failed to see how this chimney could help us, but
I didn't like to say so. Smoking sure wasn't helping
his complexion, either. He had three pimples on his
chin and one on his nose. I kept my dignified silence.

'What they done with their grandma is nothing to
do with this. But the guy who's in it now is something
else again. Big-time, very big-time sport, everyone
reckons who knows him. Just back from Aussie where

he played just about everything, but mainly rugby league.'

'Then why is he in the granny flat?' asked Lavender, sounding more than a little annoyed, probably because she wasn't up with this hot item of news. 'Sure he doesn't wet his pants?'

'Don't be stupid, Lav,' said her brother. 'Someone said he boozes a bit and he's over the hill sports-wise.'

Lavender flipped a pancake. This was one of those things she was very good at. Pancakes were her big cooking thing and she was training me to make them and to flip them. A quite marvellous woman, Lavender. 'So what makes you think he'd want to help us kids?' she asked.

'Nothing at all, really. Except your Maggie's sister, Jill, told me that her Mum was sick as hell of him lounging round all day, doing nothing, drinking and going nowhere.' He looked at his sister. 'Seems a good enough way of life to me.' Carlos smirked at both of us. 'She got rid of the old lady, see. Now she wants to get rid of her brother, or whatever he is, too.'

'Carlos, my dear, even you should know that everyone alive needs personal space for their own growth,' said Lavender. She served a pancake.

She gave me the first one. It was surely delicious.

'Well, she can't bump him out, see,' said Carlos. 'He's her own brother, and Jill reckons he put up the cash for the flat.'

It was time for me to speak. 'Quite frankly, this is leading us nowhere. Nowhere at all. You reckon some drunk lives in a flat. Some big guy in sport. He's supposed to help us?' I shoved more pancake in my mouth. 'I . . . I . . . er, ugh, er . . .'

'Don't speak with your mouth full, Tom-tit,' said

37

Carlos. He lit his third cigarette and I was delighted to hear him cough. In my experience, that's what happens to smokers. 'Where's my pancake?' he demanded.

Lavender gave him one and he smoked and ate at the same time, which is one of the most truly disgusting things ever.

'Get this mess cleaned up,' said Carlos to Lavender. 'Mummy and Jack-and-the-Beanstalk will be home any time.'

'Up your nose, too,' said his sister.

Which just about finishes one of the sadder and wetter days of my life so far. Why, why, oh why hadn't I accepted dear Mr Crow's very kind offer to be an emergency? Best place for me in any team would be if I never got called on to play.

Why? Well, who on earth wants to be on the sideline of life when the game's out there in all its glory and plonk in the middle of the field?

But, 32–0?

CHAPTER FOUR

IN WHICH WE SORT OF
BATTLE ON

Getting that team together had not been easy. While we had Ms Hennessey, our coach of sorts, she had made it very, very clear that the real work was up to us.

'I promise you, pets. I really was doing no more than cough. Wrong time, eh? Story of my life – and see where it lands me! You get your team together, give me a call and let me have a list of your rehearsal times.'

'They're not called rehearsals,' said Lavender.

'I promise I'll be there,' said Ms Hennessey.

Boggy did one of his fancy notices and we stuck it on the student noticeboard. 'Wanted! You are Wanted!!! Greenhill Soccer Team C.' Then a couple of smoking pistols. 'The Team to be Part Of. Let's Show 'em our Stuff. Join our Team if you've not had Enough!!!' Then a couple of pictures of great soccer stars. Then, 'Applications in Writing or Otherwise to L. Gibson, T. Colman or B. Lupescu before Friday. Come on, You Lot. Get into Unisex Soccer and Have a Ball.'

We had no applications. None at all. We even got hold of most of those who had been at the soccer meeting and hadn't made a team.

'Nah. Into hockey now, man.'

39

'Nuthin wrong with being an emergency. At least it's for a proper team.'

'You won't catch me dead in the same team as Lavender Gibson!'

'My Mum won't let me play with Lavender Gibson.'

'It's sure one dumb idea, anyway.'

On the second day the notice wasn't even there any longer. Ripped down? Stolen? Sabotage? Mr Crow?

'It's sheer jealousy,' said Lav.

'It can't be, Lav,' said Boggy. 'What's there to be jealous of? Anyone who wants can make our team. We'd take anyone.'

'What about all those guys out there, like us?' I said. 'All those who've never been asked to be in anything? I reckon all it needs is a personal approach.'

'Yes,' said Lavender. 'All we need to find is two each.'

'Then we still only got nine,' said Boggy.

'Isn't that enough? There's nine in a team. I know that.' It is hard to believe that in those far-off and carefree days this is what Lavender thought.

Boggy and me looked at each other. 'It'd be a start, Lav,' I said.

Then we had a massive breakthrough. A gift from God. A mass walkout of the emergencies from Team B. We netted four of them. Nick, Gordon, Brian and Wilson. 'Yeah, well, we turned out for our first practice. Eleven in the team and twenty-seven emergencies and we was near the bottom of them. Old Crow gave none of us a turn. Not once. This guy who played last year said not to hold our breath waiting. Old Crow didn't even look at us. We reckon even you lot must be better than that.'

To be absolutely honest they were not at all impressive, these four. As Lavender said in that way that she has, 'They'd better not hold their breaths waiting to turn into Diego Maradona, either.'

We were seven. Then we got Peter and Paula. They were twins and new at the school. Lav got them before anyone else had a chance to talk to them on their first day. She convinced them, in a few well chosen words, that our team was where the action was. They were properly grateful like all new kids are when they're given a bit of attention.

We were nine. Then we were ten. Lavender instructed her best friend, Maggie, to play. Trust Lav to have a friend who was the exact opposite of herself. Maggie Smith. The very pits, in my humble opinion. Probably the daughter Mrs Poppy Gibson had once dreamed of having. A very suitable sister for Carlos Gibson. A very unlikely friend for Lav. Maggie Smith dressed in pink. Pink everything. I reckon if you dug into Maggie Smith you'd find she was pink right through. Maggie was going to be an air hostess. If she couldn't be that she'd be a hairdresser. It was Lav's intention to be a radical feminist plumber.

Maggie Smith's hair was a sort of frosty blonde at the sides and pink up on top. When we had all started school together years and years ago Maggie's hair had been brown. Sure wasn't these days. She spoke like a baby and wouldn't sound the letter 'r' in any word she came across.

Maggie Smith was not a likely soccer player, but Lav gave her no choice. I have no evidence at all but have always felt that Lav had some sort of influence over Maggie, a bit like a snake charmer has over a snake. Either this or she blackmailed her.

'She doesn't know one end of a soccer ball from another,' said Bog.

'To the best of my knowledge, a soccer ball doesn't have ends,' said Lavender.

But the master stroke was mine. Dwayne Spinks. The Griller. Wow! Why no one had ever thought of Griller Spinks for a sports team before I'll never know. 'He'll kill 'em,' I said.

'Which is exactly why no one has ever thought of him before,' said Lavender. 'Think of your sporting principles.'

'I'm thinking of winning,' I said. I knew it was getting to me.

'Tom's got a point,' said Boggy, reasonably.

'Victory at any price. Is it worth it?' asked Lavender.

All this, of course, was before the days of 32–0. On that day the killing had all gone radically wrong and back to front. 'You leave Griller to me,' I said.

'You're welcome, doll,' said Maggie. 'Who ever would have thought that I'd end up playing games with Gwiller Spinks?' She shuddered in her pink and delicate way and her hair bobbed around like candy-floss in a candy-floss machine. 'Do I weally, weally have to play, Lavender? What next, sweetie?'

It was wise of them to leave Griller to me. Never hard to find Griller. Griller's territory at the school was the toilet blocks, the loos. He hung out around one or the other at all breaks, lunch times and quite often during school itself. He had no mates. None at all. Sometimes he'd order some poor kid to sort of stay with him and be his henchman for a while. Usually, however, Griller worked alone.

Griller was busy hanging a smaller kid when I found him. This was Griller's favourite sport and physical activity. He truly loved it.

Our cloakbays have rows and rows of coathooks. Quite high on the walls. No one in their right minds ever left a coat or a bag on one of these hooks if they ever wanted to see them again. There were plenty of hooks for Griller to use.

Griller would lift his victim up and hang him by his belt or the top of his pants from one of these hooks. Then he would stand back and enjoy the struggles. Sounds simple to escape, but you just try getting off a coathook. If you're just hanging there your weight sure tightens up your jeans and you're in bad, bad danger of ending up with a squeaky voice for good. I know. It's happened to me.

It's only when Griller's hung you that you find out who your real friends are. If you call and they come they're likely to end up the next ones hanging. You can count your friends on much less than the fingers of one hand. Lavender had rescued me once, though. Not even Griller took on Lavender.

'Hi there, Grill,' I called brightly as if he was the one person I had been waiting to see all day. 'How's it goin?'

'Piss off,' said Griller.

'Tom, Tom, Tom. Gemme down, Tom. Gemme down. Please. It's killing me.' A sort of squeaky voice.

Sometimes, as they say, there are moral dilemmas to be faced. Here I was, wanting a favour from Grill. There was this smaller kid, hung, turning rather red and in a bit of distress. What to do? Risk a rescue? Lose Griller? End up hanged myself?

First things first. I looked well away from the eyes of the little kid. After all, one hanging wasn't going to completely wreck him. Who knows? If I managed to spark a long-term and on-going soccer interest in Griller, I'd be saving hundreds of kids from similar disaster. I was doing the right thing by looking away.

'Grill. I gotta proposition to put to you.'

'Still 'ere? Piss off.'

'D'you want to play on our soccer team, Grill?' This was likely the very first time anyone, anywhere, had asked Griller to join in a game or be on a team. The sheer surprise would surely work.

'Piss off,' he said again.

'We'd really like to have you.'

'You deaf? You 'eard me,' Griller did not have a wide range of conversation.

'Aw, Grill. Come on. Give it a go.'

'Yeah? What's it worth?'

I did a little mental toss-up. 'I'll give you five bucks each time we play a Saturday.' What the hell, I needn't tell Lav.

As I say, sheer surprise can work like a real charm. 'Okay,' he said. 'Five bucks, then.' He grinned a wicked grin. 'Make it ten.'

'Haven't got that much, Grill. Honest. Can't get blood out of a stone.' The sight of the hanging kid out of the corner of my eye told me Griller probably could.

'Whaddya wan' me to play?'

'Keeper. Goal keeper.'

'Wanna go in the scrum.'

'Don't have scrums. That's not soccer, Grill.'

'Wanna mix it in the scrum like on telly.'

Just how much do we have to thank television for? I thought of soccer and how the rules just might be able to be bent a bit to cater for Griller Spinks' tastes. It was going to be hard. 'You can mix it in the goal, Grill. Really. I seen that on telly, too. You'll get plenty of chances in goal.' What was I doing? Where, where were all my principles of non-violence? Gone for good? 'It's real good in goal.'

'Why me in goal?' asked Griller.

44

Could I risk telling him that it was because he filled it? Filled it? He'd overflow it! 'Just, you're a natural for the goal, Grill.'

'Righto. Let's get outa here and talk about the money and when you're gonna pay it.' Grill slapped me on the back and followed through by putting his arm around me, and we headed for the door. 'Come on mate.'

'Hey, hey, hey. What about me?' Squeaking from the coathook.

'He don't want you. Piss off,' said Griller.

'I wish I could. That's what I want to do. Lemme down. Tom. Lemme down,' said the kid.

Me and my friend Griller walked out together.

We had got our team.

CHAPTER FIVE

IN WHICH I WISH I HAD THE 'FLU

When one sets out to tell a great personal story one must tell it like it is, warts and all, as the saying goes. I've heard another saying about destiny creeping up on us. If it's not destiny then it's something else that creeps up.

What crept up on me was Monday morning. The Monday morning that came right after the 32–0.

Breakfast in the Colman house. Or what passed for breakfast in the Colman house. It is one of my dearest wishes that one day we will all sit down and have a real breakfast together. A breakfast time like you see on telly, with Mum serving and everyone sitting round having waffles and pancakes and maple syrup. It's not like that with us. We eat breakfast like a relay team.

I stray from the point. Over my muesli, which Mum bought in trailer loads when it was on special at the supermarket, I said to her, 'I can't go to school today. I've got the 'flu or it could be pneumonia.'

Mum said, 'Nonsense dear. Eat your toast.'

There is no milk of human kindness in our house other than what goes on the muesli to wash it down. 'I've caught something. It was all that rain on Saturday.'

I cough very sadly. 'I think you'd better ring the school. They'd like to know what's happened to me.'

'Would they, dear?'

'My chest seems constricted by bands of iron.'

'I thought that was your mouth,' said Sue.

'That was last year, Susan, as you well know. My teeth are now perfect.'

'And I'm still paying the dentist,' said Dad.

'My health seems of very little concern to any of you. Pardon me for living. I could be dying and all I'd get from anyone here would be "eat your toast".'

'Be a waste of good bread if you were dying,' said my soulless father.

'Eat your toast, dear. Wear one of your coats today. That wind's got up again,' said Mum. 'Now, Tom, no more nonsense and please hurry up. I'm due in court at ten.'

'If you choose to put your criminal clients before your son, Mother, well, that's up to you.'

'I don't have any criminal clients, dear, as well you know. You're confusing me with someone you've read about. Or it's television again. Hurry up.'

A mother who was a lawyer, and she'd never done a juicy murder case in her whole career. It seemed there were few more boring jobs than hers. Biggest excitement we'd ever had was when she was involved in some fight between two lots of people who made toothpaste tubes, and one reckoned the other had pinched his plans. Plans? For toothpaste tubes? No wonder she was only part-time.

'I'm staying home. I have pneumonia and I think it's turning into something much worse. It's crept up on me.'

'I suggest, dear, that should you still be feeling bad at about ten you give your father a ring from the school

47

office. They won't mind, I'm sure. He'll come and collect you and take you to the doctor. That way, you won't miss out on going up on stage with all the sports captains to tell the school your team score. Will you, dear?' said my mother.

The milk of human kindness that had not gone on the muesli had gone down the drain.

'Tee, hee, hee,' said Sue.

Dad smiled. 'Come on, son. I'll drop you off on my way. I'm going over to that new subdivision on the Heights.'

Once Dad had been a builder. Now he checked the buildings other people built. He worked for the City Council.

'If I do die today, and it's quite likely, I'd like Lavender to have my grey gabardine coat, the first one I got. Boggy is to have my dinner suit. And I'm sure I can rely on the three of you to fight over the rest. You won't forget?' I said.

'Of course not, dear,' said Mum.

'I say we should let Bogdan and Lav have the lot,' said Sue. 'It'd save us the trip to the dump.'

Now that we are in our no-rugby days, soccer gets top spot at our school. Mr Harvey says, 'And now we'll hear from the school teams,' and he means soccer. Actually he means rugby under another name. It is the highlight of our Monday assemblies in winter.

Big assembly. Everyone there and the staff like a circle of owls, or hawks, on the stage.

'Come on, captains. Don't let us forget we have three this season.'

There is a glinty little look coming from the stage and I sense a feeling of big excitement coming from the audience. They all know, of course. Of course they do. It seems to me that what they want now is to watch the Christians actually being fed to the lions, and to see a bit of blood.

'Greenhill Team A. Mr Crow's team,' announces Mr Harvey. 'Come on lad. Give us your score and report. Andrew, isn't it?' He gets the name right.

Andrew, the Big-I-Am, Carlos Gibson of the future and captain of everything. Some get life given to them on a plate and then go back for pudding as well. 'Greenhill A played Western Valley A. We all had a decent game played with good sportsmanship and we beat Western Valley A, 4–1.' Big applause. 'But we all know they enjoyed it as much as we did.'

Lies! Lies! I want to scream.

He goes on. 'John Blake scored one very magnificent goal for which he was nicely set up by Nigel. Good work, John, and well done, Nigel. It's great to have such fine players in our team.' Little cough. Then to the main point. 'I scored the other three goals.' Very loud applause.

'Well done. Well done, indeed Andrew. That's what it's all about. Well done, Mr Crow, too. Good start to the season. George. Your turn now,' said Mr Harvey.

'Greenhill Team B played Greenhill High Junior grade who are bigger than us and older than us and we won 2–1 and I scored both goals.' Big, big applause.

'My word. Giant-killers, eh, Mr White?' said Mr Harvey. 'Good work, boys. Let's have a big hand for them both. What an opening to the season! Off you go now and sit down again. Really look forward to hearing from you next week. More success, I'd think. Right. What's our last song, Miss Drummond?'

God had answered my prayers. He had answered them, but Mr Crow interfered. He leaned over to his boss and said, 'I understand we have our third team,

49

Mr Harvey. Mustn't forget Miss Hennessey's team. Can't leave them out.'

'Goodness me, of course we can't,' said Mr Harvey. He looked over his glasses and spotted me. 'Come on, John. Sorry about this. Forgot all about you.'

My pneumonia was now gnawing away at my guts well and truly. Well, let the lions have their blood. Give them their meal. 'Greenhill Team C,' I began, sounding just like one of Griller's hanged victims, 'played their first game. In a new and radical approach we call total soccer we met St Joseph's, the giant-killers we all know them to be . . .'

'Giant-killers? They bottomed out last year. Only about thirty boys in the whole school.' I knew it was Mr Crow gossiping to Mr White over on the side of the stage.

'Our team,' I continued, 'performed bravely and enjoyed the excellent experience that I'm sure we all gained from the experience and made several good sporting friendships during the game. We owe a great debt of gratitude to our coach, Ms Hennessey, who is sitting here behind me and who generously provided us with our jerseys because we weren't allowed to use the school ones. We look forward to next Saturday because we have a bye.'

'Thank you. Thank you, Don. Right. A good start indeed,' said Mr Harvey.

God was on my side again until a very brave voice called out from the back of the hall. I think I spotted who it was and made a little mental note to have a chat with my new friend, Griller, later on. Hanging is too good for some people. 'He hasn't said the score, Mr Harvey.'

'Score? Oh. Thank you, lad. Don? The score?'

No use mumbling. They all knew it anyway. Here goes, pneumonia and all. 'Our score was 32–0 to St Joseph's.'

There was a little pause. Then a little buzz of sound. Murmurs drifted across the sea of heads. Then there was a sort of gargle. Then a gurgle and a slight choking chuckle that built up like a surfing wave before the wipe-out.

Then the wipe-out. The roar of wave upon wave of good solid laughter. Laughter. Cruel and heart-wrenching. The laughter of just about eight hundred laughers. Less, of course; just about ten non-laughers cowering down there somewhere. Oh would that we, too, could have been on the side of the laughers instead of being the laughees!

I suppose all good things have to come to an end. Mr Harvey and the teachers who were on duty in the hall brought the crowd back to order. 'Isn't it rather nice for us to start the week off with a good laugh?' said Mr Harvey. 'A good and happy laugh. Back to your seats, boys. Good luck for your next games.'

If it did nothing else it did provide us with our turning point.

We had a team meeting in the library after school. We all turned up. Even Griller. Even Ms Hennessey.

'I move we disband the team,' I said. 'We've made our point.'

'What point?' asked Lavender.

'I vote we give up,' said Peter.

'We never knew it was going to be like this when you asked us,' said Paula.

'No, we didn't,' said both at once. 'We don't think this is where it's all at. You tricked us into it, Lavender Gibson.'

'I never wanted to play in the first place,' said Maggie. 'It weally wecked my eyelashes on Saturday, in all that wain.'

Griller said nothing. He sat, staring out a window, chewing on a ball of gum as large as his fist and blowing balloons of it that stuck to the glass.

Ms Hennessey knitted.

'I don't really have the time. You know that,' said Boggy.

Gordon and Nick, Brian and Wilson just sat and nodded at everything. 'Being twenty-sixth emergency might not be so bad after all. Still, I reckon they won't let us back in, even at that,' said Gordon.

'I wouldn't blame them,' said Ms Hennessey, jabbing her ball of homespun very hard with both knitting needles. It was at that moment that she took charge. Well, took charge as much as anyone like Ms Hennessey ever takes charge of anything.

Everyone turned towards her. She got up, wandered to the front of the room and perched on a desk. She sure looked one superb woman in her German Army Surplus great-coat, and purple tracksuit pants and sneakers. 'You kids got yourselves into this and you can't get out of it now. So, shut your snivelling and put your money where your big mouths are.'

'He only gave me five bucks. Five bucks is all.' Even Griller's attention was taken.

'Yep. I know,' said Ms Hennessey. 'And you can damn well give it back, Dwayne. This is no time or place for standover tactics.'

'Eh?' said Dwayne.

'Shut up, Dwayne. And all of you. Now, you lot, you listen to me.' This was a new Ms Hennessey. 'I didn't ask to be here. I don't want to be here. But I am here. Mistake or not, here I am. What the hell d'you kids think you're playing at? And what the hell d'you think my life's been like today in that damned staff-room, and all because of you?'

'I don't think you should swear at us, Ms Hennessey,' sniffed Maggie.

'Swear at you, duckie? I haven't started swearing at you yet,' said the new Ms Hennessey. 'You wait till I really get going.'

This made Griller really prick up his ears.

'I am your coach. And, Tom, I would have been, even if I hadn't coughed. I was on the point of offering. I really admired you for having the guts to do something about a situation you thought was unfair and wrong. And it was, *is* wrong. Sport around here, around most schools, really stinks. If you're not a natural sport you don't get a look in. Kids like you lot never get a decent go.' She swung her legs and eyed us all up and down. 'I know you won't believe me, but you're dead lucky. I haven't been teaching long, but already I've seen the harm it can do to those who are the good ones. They're treated like little tin gods, and that's only the start. To what point? Answer me that, if you can.'

No one spoke.

'All I could see was that one or two of you thought it was time to have a bit of a nibble at what you thought was a very sweet cake. You wanted your fair share of it, too. And to do that, you found you had to take on the system. Something like that . . .' She petered out.

'You put that very well, Ms Hennessey,' said Lav. 'It's what I've always said myself.'

'I don't think you have, Lavender. But it doesn't really matter. It's my opinion that kids of your age shouldn't even be in organised teams in the stupid sock-it-to-them, slug-it-out way that you are. Kill 'em and win at all costs. It's bad. All you do is give a helluva lot of oldies, parents and teachers, second-hand kicks.' She was quiet for just a moment. 'But that's beside the point, now. You got into it. You stay in it. I don't care if you lose every game 32–0, you'll see out the competition. Then you can make up your minds. Right?'

Not a sound.

Ms Hennessey picked up a very strange ally. 'Yeah. Ms Hennessey is right,' Griller spoke. 'I liked it on Saturday.'

'Don't be silly, Griller,' said Ms Hennessey, forgetting to use his right name. 'You only lasted two seconds and I've got a feeling you might have been banned for life.'

'Yeah, but,' said Griller, 'I went and looked at this other game after that. It was good, eh? Know what I gotta do now more'n what Tom reckoned from watching that stupid video.'

'I take your point, Dwayne,' said Ms Hennessey, the real teacher. 'You can be assured that I am now going to be in charge. I've got to find you a coach. I can't be a real coach. And, Tom, no more of this silly nonsense of total radical soccer and learning a game by watching *Match of the Day* on telly. No matter how much of the best you watch you still must learn to walk before you run. In truth, you've got to learn how to get your feet to make contact with the ball.'

Maggie, Lavender and me told her all about Maggie's uncle in the granny flat and she said, 'I can't understand what makes you think he'd be of any use or even want to help. Still, any port in a storm so I'll give him a call.'

'What about your guy, Mitch?' asked Boggy.

'My guy Mitch knows as much about soccer as most of you,' said Ms Hennessey. She must have thought she'd let him down a bit because she added, 'Still, he's good at other things.'

'I'll bet,' growled Griller.

'When I grow up I fully intend having a house-husband, too,' said Lav to me. 'Must be real good.'

'You kids have got just under two weeks to get your act together. Somehow or other, and I make you this promise, you're going to do it,' said Ms Hennessey. All of a sudden it struck me that she sounded for all the world like Mr Crow. All teachers are tarred with the same brush under the skin, I thought to myself.

CHAPTER SIX

IN WHICH WE MAKE A NEW FRIEND

Slipping almost undetected through the pages of this tale, dear readers, is the person of my very good and lifelong friend, Bogdan Lupescu of Central Europe, Sydney Australia and our suburb. He comes from the wild country of Rumania, from a spot not far from where the great Count Dracula, of massive bloody fame, lived in days gone by and, it is said, still lives today.

Lupescu means something like wolf and I have this feeling that Boggy may indeed be connected, by blood, with the Dracula family. Bog will never confirm or deny this. As yet I haven't managed to get up the courage to ask his father, Mr Lupescu, who is big in Central European trade and sells us railway engines, caviar and shotguns. I have noted, however, that both Boggy and his father have rather large teeth.

Boggy's been my close friend for years, and I have a feeling the Central Europeans intend leaving the Lupescus here, or have forgotten them or something like that. Mrs Lupescu is an Australian and may not be fully welcome back in the Dracula country of Transylvania. I've not exactly asked her but this is Lavender's opinion.

Bog and me were closer in the far-off pre-Lavender days, but we still get together whenever we can or whenever Lavender lets us. The love of a good woman may be something special, but it sure tends to rob you of your men friends. I've told Lav that one day Boggy will be best man at my wedding. She says that's okay by her, but don't expect her to turn up. Lavender says the days of getting married are truly over and it's nothing but a con on the part of men who want free housekeepers. She reckons her place will never be under the thumb of a man. Stay single, is Lav's advice, and the only way the human race can be saved. I can think of some very good reasons why Lav's methods may spell the end of the human race. She says that's a load of bull and that science and test tubes will enable the creation of life to go on and without any of the mess.

'Without any of the fun, either,' my Dad said when I told him. 'Don't know where that kid gets her ideas. It's sure not from her mother.'

'She reads widely,' I said.

There is one other big reason, apart from Lav, why me and Boggy have grown apart. Bogdan Lupescu is a child prodigy. I have told him that at the age of thirteen he should call himself a young adult prodigy but he reckons it's not the same thing. Being a kid gets you further as a prodigy. There are lots of young adult ones and very few kids.

Bog plays the piano. Not just *Chopsticks*, either. It's not for Boggy to discover what he wants to be by trying out a few things along the way. It's all been set for him for just about nine years already. He's going to play the piano all over the world, make his fortune and become famous very quickly. I think he's got to make Mrs Lupescu's fortune, too. Both she and Mr Lupescu have a big stake in poor old Bog.

Since Boggy was four years old, he's had to get up at six in the morning and work at playing the piano. Even had to do it when his legs were little and he couldn't give his feet a rest on the pedals. It's still six in the morning and another two or three hours after school. His piano teacher? You've guessed it! Mrs Lupescu. In the olden days back in Sydney she was once a piano player herself.

What surprises and amazes me is that Boggy really likes it. Probably this amazing thing comes from being an only child and not being exposed to the true world like the rest of us. If it's not that, it's because he's dreaming of all the money he's going to make.

He's going to play with the Regional Symphony Orchestra this year. It's what he calls his debut. A debut, for Bog, is a sort of opening concert in the long, long piano playing career ahead of him. He is playing a very long concerto by Mozart. I know it's long because I've listened to him playing it, and it takes just about forever. It sure has a lot of notes in it.

'He's the young Mozart. Our own young Mozart,' Mrs Lupescu told me.

I told Mrs Lupescu that the young Mozart composed his first opera, or something like that, at the age of seven or eight and that Boggy was leaving it a bit late. Mrs Lupescu didn't invite me back for about a month after that.

It is something of a pity that Boggy's piano playing debut and his soccer debut have kind of clashed and coincided.

Mrs Smith's brother in the granny flat clearly hadn't stood a chance with Ms Hennessey.

'Alf's agreed to take you under his wing, pets,' she cried. We were out on the field that the new and assertive Ms Hennessey had told Mr Crow to get off otherwise she'd take the matter up with Mr Harvey and then with her union. Alf was right behind her and poor Mr Crow clearly didn't see that he had much option.

Alf made Griller look like a peanut. He was gross. Real gross. If Eugene, the next Mr Poppy Gibson, was two metres high, then Alf was just about two metres wide. It struck me that the two of them would make a great combination for something. I couldn't think what.

Alf stood for no nonsense. Not now. Not ever. No how. 'Right, youse lot. Someone set me up for this and somehow I've let meself get talked into this pansy set-up. This little lady, here, done it, I think,' he hung an arm around Ms Hennessey's shoulders and she didn't seem to mind. Goodness knows what Mitch would have thought.

'Sharlene, here,' – he patted Ms Hennessey – 'tells me I've gotta turn youse into something.' He spat. He sure could spit. 'I'm resting between jobs meself just at the mo, so it seems I've landed meself right in the . . .' He caught Ms Hennessey's eye.

'Mr Smith has very kindly offered his services to help you. To help our cause, pets. Now, it so happens to transpire . . .'

'It wha'?' asked Mr Smith.

'It seems that Mr Smith has never played soccer, but that doesn't really matter.'

'Playin' league these last seven years Sydney-side,' said Alf. 'Big bucks.'

'Tough game,' I said, nicely.

'Shut up, kid,' said Alf. 'Speak when you're spoken to.'

'Yes,' I said. Then added, 'Sir.'

Alf lifted his hand. It was the size of a leg of lamb. 'Din'ya hear me, kid?'

'Alf,' said Ms Hennessey. 'Remember the wee chat we had last night about how we handle young adolescents?'

'Loadabull,' said Alf. 'Let's get down to it. Gotta learn a bit meself about this 'ere pansy game. Girlies' game, ask me.' He glanced down at Maggie, Lavender and Paula. 'Youse three in the right place, eh? Gawd knows what's wrong with the resta ya. Ask me ya haven't got no . . .'

'Alf,' warned Ms Hennessey.

'Well, reckon they haven't. Still.'

Griller spoke. An unwise move on his part. 'Think I might give soccer a miss.' Then he added, 'Sir.' He got to his feet.

'Siddown!' A very big roar.

Griller did.

'I consider the methods you are using, Mr Smith, are not really . . .' started Lavender.

'You, too!' he roared.

Then he killed us. He was right, quite right to say we were not physically fit. Having said it, he then started to do something about it. We ran, we jumped. We ran, we bobbed up and down. We ran, we stretched. We ran. We ran. He put us through ten times as much as his mates on the Sydney-side rugby league team had ever had to do. And then some. Somehow, we all did it. Somehow, funnily, we didn't seem to mind. He did it with us. So, too, did Ms Hennessey. A whole hour; more, and we didn't even touch a ball.

60

In the end he let us go.

'Same time. Same place. Tomorrer!' he roared.

'I don't think we'll be able to get these grounds to-morrow,' said Ms Hennessey.

'That squint little feller want 'em, eh?' asked Alf. 'We'll see about that. Same time tomorrer. Right? Now youse lot, get the hell out of it. Me and this little lady's goin' for a drink.' He draped his arm around Ms Hennessey again and they took off in her van.

'Mum'll kill me. I've got to get home,' said Bog.

He had a point. Mrs Lupescu was noted for her fiery Rumanian temper even though she was an Aussie. She could be a sort of female Alf, but a lot smaller.

Which left me and Griller and Lavender. A sort of an odd trio. We walked home together.

'That ape's not gonna tell me whadda do,' said Griller, sounding like Alf already.

'Yes he is, Dwayne,' said Lavender.

'Like hell he is,' said Dwayne, as nicely as possible.

'I am perfectly sure he is anti-feminist, absolutely sexist and a fascist pig. He's out of the ark,' said Lav.

'Eh?' said Dwayne. 'Thought he said he was from Sydney.'

'And,' Lav started slowly. 'I can tell he's absolutely all man. All man.'

There was a strange sound to this bit. She sounded just like Mrs Poppy Gibson talking about Eugene. 'What on earth do you mean?'

'I'm all man, too,' said Griller.

'Dwayne, my dear,' said Lavender. 'Compared to Alf you're just a little boy. Why, while you still enjoy picking the wings off flies Alf's out big-game hunting.'

'Uh?' enquired Griller.

'All I'm saying is that was the most invigorating hour I've spent for many a long day,' said Lavender. 'And

I simply must speak to Mummy about getting me a decent tracksuit from the shop. Come on now, Tomtit, and stop tripping over that dreadful coat.' She smiled. 'I must admit that Alf's ideas are more than a little radical. Still, you can't deny that total soccer may just about be on our horizon.'

A truly depressing sight faced me as I took stock of myself in front of the bathroom mirror. If ever there was a need for prayers to be answered, there it was staring right at me.

I have always said that looks, good looks, are nothing. What is inside the package is what counts. No one ever worries about the wrapping. It always gets chucked away. Oh, how I've lied to myself.

I put myself in a mental row of those men who were best-known to me. What cruel punishment. Indeed, hidden away among them all I could hardly spot myself. What chance, then, of anyone else spotting me?

There they all were. Eugene, the next Mr Poppy Gibson. Two metres of him and still probably growing because men don't stop their growing until they're about twenty-eight. I read that in the *Reader's Digest*. Just look at Eugene. Two metres of superb sporting machine. Not much conversation in him, it is true. But, who the hell needs conversation when you're like that? Where had conversation ever got me? Never got me anywhere and I had boxes of it. Eugene! He'd even won the hand of Mrs Poppy Gibson. A much older lady, of course, but still of great charm and ability, for all her advancing years. Quite a goer, as they say.

Eugene's soon-to-be stepson, Carlos. All Swedish blond good looks in spite of the fact that he was Portuguese and the son of the first Mr Poppy Gibson. Carlos da Souza he had been back in the days before Mrs Poppy Gibson changed all their names back to the one she had before she got into marrying. Lavender once told me Carlos wasn't even his real name. His real name was Jesus. A common name for the Portuguese, but your non-Portuguese never say it right. Haysus is the way you say it. I tried it out on him once and he knocked me to the ground. The handsome, if somewhat thick, Carlos.

Lavender was Mrs Poppy Gibson's English rose. Her father, the second Mr Poppy Gibson, or so Lav said, was an old English aristocrat called Mr Aubrey Hilton-Styles. One day, she said, he would come back to claim her, and to take her to some large estate of land and a castle that belonged to her back in England. My Mum said this was all news to her. He was no big aristocrat, he was a seaman who jumped ship out here so he could marry Mrs Poppy Gibson. He jumped back on double quick when he found out what she was like. Mum said she should know; she was Mrs Poppy Gibson's witness at the Post Office wedding.

And now there was Alf. Line him up too. Not quite so much your traditional American-type stud. In fact more of an ugly hunk, come to think of it, but possessed, quite clearly, of great animal magnetism and power, and quite a way with the ladies.

Boggy? Of course the family connection to Count Dracula must help, even if it only meant good, strong teeth. Could hardly stack Boggy up with Alf and Eugene and Carlos, but he still had a good half a head start on me. Add to that the world fame that will soon be at his feet, and it is a truly depressing thought.

Griller Spinks? No. Not quite. Still, even old Grill had something. Not much, but something. And wouldn't it be nice, just once in a while, to have the power to hang a person of your choice from a cloakbay coathook?

Dad? Stretching it a bit. Still, it shows the depths to which I am sunk when even the elderly have it all over me. My Mum once told me that Dad looked just like me when he was a kid and it was a miracle of nature when, all of a sudden, at about eighteen, he just blossomed forth into what he became. I never thought he blossomed into very much but they do say love is blind.

There they were. Lined up behind me in the mirror. And there was me. So much nothing, you couldn't see me. No moustache. Next to no hair anywhere except on the head. A walking disaster of little muscle, little size and no animal attraction.

'If you don't get the hell out of that bathroom, I'm going to axe the door,' yelled Dad. Which summed up the amount of sympathy and understanding I ever got in that house.

'You have told me, Father, that cleanliness is next to godliness,' I said.

'Yes,' said my father. 'And like everything else you do you've taken it to excess. Get out of there and dry the dishes and haven't you got any homework?'

The great peoples of North America employ people they call personal analysts. You go to them to pour out your troubles. Well, I want one. I need one in order to report on my very stink family.

'Well, sweetheart, how was the practice?' asked Mum.

'Okay.'

'Tell us about it. How was Maggie's uncle as a coach?'

Sometimes they must know everything. 'Okay, I guess. Mind you, I still say my methods would've worked if we'd given them a real chance. It's just that I wasn't blessed with a team of any ability at all.'

'You!' said Sue, sticking her nose in. 'You were lucky to be blessed with any team at all. They must be mad to follow you.'

'Leave Tom alone, Sue. I think he's doing a great job,' said Mum. 'Just one or two lessons for him to learn, that's all.'

Do you ever get over learning lessons? 'Yeah,' was all I said.

'And you must face it, dear,' she went on, 'it was rather doomed to failure. A book on the game and a video of some match. No matter how good, they're not quite the same as getting stuck in and doing some work on whatever skills are needed.'

'Yeah.'

'It's certainly true that you weren't blessed with too likely a team, but you mustn't blame them for that. I just think it's great that you've opened up things to so many who hadn't had a chance to try them before.'

'Yeah.'

'Make us a cup of tea, dear,' she said. 'And, I must say, you've taught me a lesson, too.'

'I have?' This sounded a bit better.

'Yes you have. You and all your friends going to all this trouble. I think it's time us parents got in behind and lent a little support. You know. Come and see you play. You just wait. We'll all be there the next time you play. Mark my words.'

All well and good. We might be a weird team but we've got even weirder parents.

CHAPTER SEVEN

IN WHICH OUR NEW FRIEND
SEEMS TO SCORE

Wednesday. Second practice. Lavender wore a pink tracksuit and pink sneakers. 'It's not pink, Tommy. It's cerise. It's this year's fashion colour and it's the last one Mummy had in stock. She's getting me the headband to go with it.'

Ms Hennessey wore a pale green tracksuit with darker green footwear. Her big mop of radical red hair was tied back with a matching green ribbon.

Maggie was in her usual baby pink with a white stripe, and Paula's tracksuit was in a deep cream colour.

Alf didn't wear very much at all. Just an old T-shirt that had once been white and on which you could still read 'I'm yours for the asking.' He wore pink shorts and had bare feet. None of the guys had bothered to change, though I noticed Griller wearing a coat from the Presbyterian Ladies. One of their new load.

We were in the gym. Clearly, when Alf and Ms Hennessey put their minds together they are a force to be reckoned with. It seemed we could have the gym on Mondays and Wednesdays, and have whatever field we liked on Tuesdays and Thursdays. Alf was going to let us have a rest on Fridays.

'And if youse lot don't do no good by me on Sat'dy youse got a ten-mile run on Sund'y.' Alf was very non-metric. 'And I done me homework, see. From this book your Miss Hennessey give me. Got caught up on all them skills this here pansy game needs. Let's get to work.'

We worked out for half an hour. Fitness. I think it meant we would either end up fit or dead. 'Mr Smith, you'll kill us,' said Lav.

'Call me Alf, kid. All youse can call me Alf. Kill ya? Might not be such a bad idea, lookin' at youse all.'

'Uncle Alf, Mum says I've got to be home before five,' said Maggie.

'Leave ya Mum to me,' said Alf. 'And do six press-ups for answering me back.'

'I didn't answer you back, Uncle Alf.'

'Do ten,' he roared. 'We're all here till half four 'cept for little Poppitoffski who has to go play the pianner.'

We did little hopping dances and little side-step dances and little bobbing dances. We did them by ourselves and we did them with a partner. We did sit-ups, pull-ups and turn-you-inside-out-ups.

Alf and Ms Hennessey had found half a dozen practice balls and we all got into kicking and dribbling and volleying. If fitness was bad, this was worse. We worked our butts off by ourselves and then with our partners.

'We 'ardly started but that's enough for today,' yelled Alf. 'Your Miss Hennessey's got yer homework for yer. Give it out, Shar.'

Ms Hennessey gave us each a copy of the rules of the game. 'Alf says you've got to know all these by tomorrow because he's going to give you a test. I did try to tell him we didn't do things that way these days, but . . .'

'I said to 'er what was good enough for me was good enough for youse lot. Ten laps of the field if youse don't get ten outa ten. Okay?'

Us poor, silly, dumb sheep just sat there smiling and nodding as he laid out the rules for our slaughter. Most of us said, 'Thanks, Alf.'

'Out! The lot of youse. Scram. Me and Sharlene's goin' to the pub. Come on, Shar.'

Ms Hennessey put on her dark green ski jacket, over which Alf draped his arm.

Lavender put on her new blue ski jacket and said, 'I do hope Mummy's got me that headband. Come on, Tommy.'

'Don't call me Tommy.'

'Tom-tit, then.'

'And definitely not that.'

'Then come on, old grumpy bones. I'll shout you a milkshake down town.'

I couldn't afford to refuse even though I wanted to. Griller hadn't paid me back my five bucks from the first game. I think I could see what he'd used it for.

'You haven't said what you think of my new gear,' said Lavender.

I couldn't resist risking the milkshake. 'If you put a bit of white fur here and there you could get a job as Father Christmas.'

'Ho, ho, ho,' said Lavender. She seemed in an excellent mood.

'Where's the woman I know who says the consumer society stinks?'

'She's . . . she's . . . I don't know,' Lavender twittered.

'Look at all that artificial fibre you're wearing,' I said. 'You and me did all that research last year on just how much of our natural resources are needed to produce

68

that rubbish. You're wearing the equivalent of a good five barrels of oil.'

'No I'm not, Tommy. I happen to be wearing a designer tracksuit. Swiss Cherry Cerise. Hundred and ninety-five bucks but less to the trade and enough to gladden the heart of any girl. Oh, Tommy, I know I can tell you. We're such close, close friends and always will be. I think I'm in love.'

We were passing the bike shed. I thought all the cares in the world were dropping from my shoulders and my heart gave a little lurch. This was it! I turned to Lav. It wasn't easy; my bike got in the way and poked me painfully just where it shouldn't. 'But . . . but . . . Lav. Why didn't you say something before. I thought . . .'

'Don't be dumb, Tommy. There hasn't been any before. I only first set eyes on him yesterday.'

'Set eyes on who?'

'On Alf, thickhead. Alf!' she cried. 'The very name does something to me, Tommy. Don't you see? He's all man, is that man.'

The cares of the world clambered back onto my shoulders. 'He's old enough to be your father,' I said. 'Who knows, he might be old enough to be your grandad.' Like mother, like daughter, only the other way round.

How could I have been so blind? Oh, God, what had I done to deserve this?

'Age has nothing to do with it. Oh, Tommy, you should have felt his hands, when he was working on me for that silly kicking exercise. There was a sense of something between us I find impossible to describe.'

'Yeah,' I said. 'It was probably the sweat on his hands. I'd be careful if I was you. I think you might have to fight Ms Hennessey for him.'

'Don't be silly, Tommy. They're just good friends

in a professional sort of way. Besides, she's got Mitch, and she can't want more than one. It's just that fate has flung them together in the fight for our soccer cause.'

'Looked like more than fate he was flinging around her, when they took off for the pub,' I said. Women! Would I ever understand the riddle of them? Fate was sure flinging something my way and it sure stank.

'Whatever happens, Tommy dear, whatever happens you will always be my very dearest friend. There will always be a special place in my heart for you.'

It is wondrous what love does. Until now Lav had always reckoned that the heart was nothing more than an outsize and very strong muscle, and its only job was to pump blood around the body. Still, what was the use of saying anything more until after we had our milkshakes?

I had a double-chocolate malted thick thickshake and Lav had a diet cola for her figure, and then we dropped by at the Poppy G. Boutique and Accessory Bar. Carlos Gibson was also there. He looked like a lizard or a skink. He was lounging half over the accessory bar and half over two of Mrs Poppy Gibson's younger customers.

'Lavender, my sweet,' cried Mrs Poppy Gibson. 'It's the first time in years I've seen you look halfway decent, and I've got that headband for you here somewhere. Darling, you look lovely. Popular line that, too. Went like hot cakes. Hello, Tom. How are you today?'

'Fine, thanks, Mrs Gibson.'

'There's lamb chops in the fridge, dear. Just for you and Carlos. I'm off to see Eugene play, and there's a nice cheesecake, too.'

'Okay, Mummy.'

'We'll go on somewhere afterwards to eat or whatever. Don't save anything or wait up, and make sure Carlos does the dishes.'

'Okay, Mummy.'

How very, very true is that old, old saying: Like mother, like daughter. Both of them well into sportsmen. Blood will out.

Mrs Poppy Gibson was certainly a most attractive older woman. She was thirty-five, and had been about this for several years, according to Lav. According to my Mum, too. She had a great quantity of white-blonde hair. Lav said it was really brown. She pulled her hair tight from her face and piled it on top of her head and then let it fall in sort of curls. She had long, long eyelashes. Lavender said they were made of a fur called sable and her mother cut them from a long roll that looked like a centipede.

Mrs Poppy Gibson's clothes were always the height of consumerism, which they had to be if she, Carlos and Lavender were to eat and pay the mortgage. She was a sort of walking advertisement for her business. Around her neck and wrists she wore truly great quantities of gold, and on her fingers was more gold and a lot of diamonds. According to Lav the gold and the rings were Mrs Poppy Gibson's insurance against hard times, old age, and not being able to pay the mortgage. My Mum said that was a load of nonsense and that the gold and rings were just trophies from the chase. Which is something that really puzzles me because Mrs Poppy Gibson seemed to have no interest in sport whatsoever, much less jogging. My Mum was her best friend and always had been. In fact she was Mrs Poppy Gibson's only woman friend due to her preferring men. They had nothing in common and very often did not 'see eye to eye', as Mum says.

My Mum and Dad were the only people who ever called Mrs Poppy Gibson by her proper name. This was Florrie. Mum and Dad were the godparents of

71

Carlos, because when he came along his mother was very religious as a result of having married a Portuguese. By the time Lav came along she had changed her religion and was a Freethinker, and poor old Lav had to put up with not being christened.

'Remind your parents of my party on Saturday week, Tommy, and keep on reminding them. I know your mother will do anything to get out of coming. It's . . . it's . . .' She looked all young and giggled, and all her gold bracelets tinkled. 'It's Eugene's and my engagement party. Isn't that a hoot? And I've said to Lavender to bring all her friends for the first couple of hours. Carlos and his friends have got the garage, and your little hockey team can scoot around till about nine or so. I want just everyone to be there,' she said.

I hoped for their sakes that she'd invite the neighbours. 'I'll tell her,' I said.

'Tell her, too, I'll pop in with that sweater she wants on my way home. It's a dreadful colour but that's so like your mother. She'll never take my advice.'

Lavender had found the headband, and was trying it on in as many ways as she could. 'Mumsy,' she called. 'Make me an appointment at Hairport for Friday, will you? I think silver streaks would be just the ticket.'

'If you say so, honey. Mind you, I think a slight pinky rinse might be just you, and would certainly spark off your new gear. Pink's just so, so *in* at the moment. All the girls are having it and I'm going to have it run through mine for the party. We'd be sisters then,' she laughed and tinkled very girlishly.

They just about made me want to spew.

I walked home with Lav. 'If you don't want your new fur coat I'll buy it off you,' I said.

'Okay,' said Lav. 'It'll cost you fifteen bucks.'

That's capitalism for you. 'I'll pay it off over three weeks,' I said.

'In that case it's another two bucks for terms,' said Lavender.

CHAPTER EIGHT

IN WHICH THERE'S A BIT
OF THIS AND THAT

It may well seem to you, dear readers, that the only thing on my mind in those far-off and golden days of just a while ago was soccer, the team, Lavender and my fast-fading love life, and the onset of my approaching manhood. How right you are.

However, to keep the record straight, I must briefly outline one or two other bits in my life during those troubled and painful days.

Home, for example. What was life truly like with a building inspector father, a part-time lawyer mother and an over-skinny sister?

School, for example. How, during these days, was I still able to produce several book reports, a science project for the science fair, model a pair of bookends in the shape of monkeys (for woodwork, even though they were sculpted in clay)? Of course I had also to play a full part in the debating club of which I am hon. sec. and number two debater. Lav is the number one debater. Just how did I manage everything that was required of me by Miss Webster, our teacher? How did I do it all? I think it was a miracle. Poor Miss Webster; she doesn't feature in the pages of this tale very much at all. And apart from this paragraph, and a passing mention here and there, she won't again. No modern Ms is our Miss Webster. She is truly elderly in a way that Mrs Poppy Gibson is not. She has grey hair and glasses, and wears grandmother-type clothing that is only a hop and skip away from ending up with the Presbyterian Ladies. She sure doesn't shop at the Poppy G. Boutique and Accessory Bar, even though Lavender has tried to encourage her by offering her a family discount.

To my simple mind Miss Webster is one of those people who truly make the world tick. She seldom raises her voice and never criticises people. She will criticise behaviour, but not people. Helpful at all times and knows her stuff as a teacher. A true saint, if somewhat boring. It's a bit of a pity I can't get her to make more of a mark on this story. Still, some things are beyond my ability even. It is absolutely unlikely that Miss Webster will be attending the Mrs Poppy Gibson and Eugene engagement party. Quite simply, we do not all move in the same circles in this less than ideal world of ours.

My parents? I know in my heart, of course, that I was not really blessed with parents who have a deep understanding of me. Another of life's little tragedies in our less than ideal world. I suppose because of their own very busy and rather selfish lives, the thought of me, forever on the sideline of life but never part of the game, does not occur to them. A pity because, I feel sure, they have very much to offer. Most kids go through a time of thinking they've been adopted and are really the child of a member of the royal family, a big-time gangster who's in prison or a movie star who doesn't want to be reminded of their past. Well, not me. I've always known whose son I am. There's a picture of Dad at home, taken when he was about my age and we could be twins. This does not fill me with great excitement because, as I've hinted before, he hasn't turned out anything spectacular.

I am afraid I must tell you that my home life is filled with drudgery. Great dollops of drudgery. My family sure don't need a servant with me about the place. I am very well used to lawn-mowing, firewood chopping, concrete sweeping, weeding and gardening, laundry and hanging out clothes, bringing in clothes and ironing, vacuuming and dusting, window cleaning, car cleaning, dish washing, dish drying, dish put-awaying. In other words, all those things that keep a family together. It hurts deeply when my parents, thoughtless as are all parents, are often heard to mutter or yell things like, 'Bone idle', or 'I'm sick to death of fetching and carrying for that kid while he can't get off his lazy fat backside.' Hurtful and untrue. It is more than a pity that my rear-end will never be fat.

It is very true, of course, that such criticisms should be levelled very loudly at my sister. While Sue may not be anorexic, she sure is double keen on staying thinner than a broom handle. Sue, the reject lover of Carlos Gibson, even though they're god-cousins. Until a while back they were one big thing. They were just so much in love with each other it made Lavender ill. They were like Siamese twins. Not any longer, however. Sue's story was that she couldn't go on loving a man who thought more of his reflection than he did of her. Personally I could only disagree. If I had a reflection like Carlos Gibson I'd sure think more of it than of my sister Susan. Lavender reckoned this wasn't the real reason behind their split. She said it was the old Eternal Triangle, and there was Another Woman and Carlos got caught out by Sue just when he least expected it. This whole thing makes no sense to me. A guy like Carlos has the ability as well as the equipment to handle not only your Eternal Triangle but anything at all up to about an Eternal Hexagon.

Now here I was, just like Sue, done in by a Gibson. Another Woman? Another Man? Same thing if you ask me. Lavender and Alf Smith, nice and comfy down on the base, and me on the apex and none too comfortable.

Readers, these few lines of insight are an effort on my part to give a fuller picture of a multi-sided life. All good things must come to an end. So, back to soccer.

'My Mum says I've got to give it away,' said Boggy.

'After nine years of practising I think that's a pity,' I said.

'Soccer, not the piano,' he said. 'It's taking far too much time and it's only five or six weeks till the debut.'

'All work and no play, Boggy,' I warned.

'It's not, is it? Like it's all play and no play,' he said.

'I'll come and see her,' I said.

'I don't think that'll work,' he said very quickly.

'Of course it will,' I replied, and I wouldn't take no for an answer.

'Hello, Tom,' said Mrs Lupescu.

'Hello, Mrs Lupescu,' I said.

'How's tricks?' she asked, nicely I thought. 'Haven't seen you round here for an age.'

I didn't like to point out to her that I hadn't felt exactly welcome since my remarks about young Mozart. 'Pretty busy with soccer,' I said.

'I've noticed,' she said, not quite so nicely. 'It's all too much for Bogdan, and he's never really been a sporty sort of boy. His music is everything to him.'

'I think it's very good of you, Mrs Lupescu, and Mr

Lupescu too, to make sure there's more to his life than just music. I think I must have discussed my ideas with you before about the all-round man.'

'I think you have, Tom,' she said quite quickly. 'And I must say I think that Bogdan's getting just a little too all-rounded at the moment.'

I knew she didn't mean his size. Bog was as thin as me, even if a bit taller. 'He's having a great time at soccer, Mrs Lupescu.'

'It's taking too much out of him, Tom. This is, well, just such an important time in his life. Everything has been done for this moment. Everything is in place for his concert.'

It was on the tip of my tongue to tell her what my Mum had said. Would it help Mrs Lupescu see things more clearly? One of Mum's favourites, about how a lot of parents get their kids to do all those things they haven't had the chance to do when they were little. Perhaps this wasn't quite the right moment.

'Seems to me, Tom, it's one thing or the other. Both are just too much,' said Mrs Lupescu.

'I wouldn't like to see Bog give up the piano after so long at it, Mrs Lupescu,' I said.

'You know I didn't mean that, Tom,' said Mrs Lupescu. I sensed a little icy tone in her voice.

'Please don't make him give up his soccer. Please, Mrs Lupescu,' I begged her. 'We really do need him.' Let's face it, replacements weren't lining up for Bog's place on the team.

Suddenly she smiled, 'If I didn't know you so well, you little devil, I'd belt you from here to kingdom come!' Then she got all serious again. 'You know how much time goes into Bogdan's music. You know that very well. You should also know that in spite of what he says to you, it means the world to him. Everything.

Well, almost everything. And I must be honest; it means a great deal to his father and me.'

Bogdan came in. He looked between me and his mother and knew what it was all about.

'It's up to Bogdan,' said Mrs Lupescu. 'It is his life. It is his time. Why, why, why,' – and she flung her arms about in great Central European fashion – 'didn't you get into soccer last year?'

'I'll cut back on soccer, Mum. I told you I would. I had a good talk to Ms Hennessey and Alf, and they agree I can play Saturdays and come twice a week to practice, and that's enough. Alf says he's looking forward to my concert because I have to be a better piano player than a soccer player.'

'He used to play the piano himself,' I said. 'Maggie told me. It was in a pub on Sydney-side. He was probably good at that, too. Can I come and hear you play now, Bog?'

While, truthfully speaking, Lav and me are into our heavy metal stage, there's just something about listening to Boggy playing Mozart. It sure soothes the jangled nerves.

Alf said, 'Got one big surprise for youse guys.' He was carrying a carton.

Friday. Three-thirty p.m. Gymnasium. Thirty hours and thirty minutes to kick-off. Countdown time to game two.

He dumped the carton. 'Sit up straight, youse fellers. Arms folded now. Still as a mouse.' He leaned back to admire us. 'Reckon as I shoulda been a teacher, eh Shar? Look at all them little sods, eh?'

'If that's the way you feel, Alfie,' she said, getting out of her dark green ski jacket. 'Most days you'd be welcome to my lot.'

'Youse lot don't give this little lady 'ere a bad time, do ya?' he roared. 'Have me to deal with if ya do, let me tell ya.'

'They're not my class, Alfie,' said Ms Hennessey. 'Only Peter and Paula, and they're no trouble at all.'

'Watcha got us then?' asked Griller, very politely.

'Shut up, kid,' said Alf and tipped the contents of the box on the floor.

Soccer shirts! Brand new! Absolutely brand new. Grass green. A proper colour and shape, everything we could have dreamed of. 'Whaddya say, eh?' he yelled.

'Alf, dear, they're wonderful. Bless you,' said Lavender the creep.

'Isn't he just a marvel, then?' said Ms Hennessey.

I had to agree. An absolute, top number, total marvel. 'Where'd you get them?' I breathed.

Alf winked hard. 'Let's just say they fell off the back of a truck,' he said.

Oh, no. Not on top of everything else. Now I'd have the worry of keeping a lookout for the cops, seeing the jerseys stripped off our backs halfway through a game. 'Back of a truck, eh?' I asked.

'Back of a truck.' Wink, wink from Alf.

Didn't seem to worry any of the others. They were into them and sorting them for size. 'Come on, cap'n.' Alf winked again. 'Try one on.'

I forgot all about certain arrest and thought my heart would burst. 'Captain?' I squeaked.

'Who else, kid? It's your team,' said Alf. 'None of us be 'ere if it wasn't for you. Mind you . . .'

He had kept this till last. What a man! All week he'd refused to say who would captain the team. All he'd say was that it'd be the one best suited to the job and anyone who asked would be clobbered.

'There's . . . there's . . .' Griller tried to get started.

80

He looked as sad as he sounded.

'Not one for you, eh? Stupid pansy game. Sure is one stupid pansy game. God knows why the goalie should 'ave a uniform different from the rest. Never understand it. Let 'im 'ave it, Shar.'

A super dark blue, roll-neck sweatshirt. Beautiful. Big as a tent. Grill's eyes shone. Not for the Grillers of this world the worry of things falling off the backs of trucks. Bless him.

Team talk. Pep talk. Good old Alf working himself into the ground just to build up our confidence. 'If youse guys don't want the feel of my boot up your bums youse'll do everything I say. Geddit?'

'Yes, Alf.' A chorus.

'Youse guys'll remember everything I taught ya. Geddit?'

'Yes, Alf.' A bigger chorus.

Before he let us go Lavender made a speech. 'On behalf of the team, Alf, may I express our gratitude for all you've done for us and Ms Hennessey, too. Well, I don't exactly mean what you've done for Ms Hennessey but what she's done for us, too.'

'Okay, kid,' said Alf.

'Where would we be without you, I ask myself?' said Lavender.

'Up the creek with no flippin' paddle,' said Alf. 'But don't you be worryin' your pretty little pink head about askin' no stoopid questions like that, honey.'

He couldn't stop Lavender. 'May I also remind all of you that it's party-time at the Gibson house tomorrow night. Be there at seven-thirty sharp and bring a bottle.'

'Yeah. Nicked me Mum's gin when you first said, Lav,' said Griller.

'And Mum says you're to come too, Alf. Only you

get to stay longer'n us. You too, Ms Hennessey. And,' Lavender smiled a sweet pink smile, 'do bring Mitch.'

'Mitch? Mitch who?' said Ms Hennessey.

'And finally,' said Lavender.

'At last,' said Griller.

'We will do our very best to win for you tomorrow, Alf.'

'Don't youse expect no miracles, kid,' said Alf. 'And youse don't do it for me. It's for yourselves and for the whole team. In this together, youse lot. Winning's not the only thing it's all about. See ya there tomorrer.'

Which I felt served to put Lavender Gibson down just a little peg. After all, truth to tell, it should have been the captain making the speech. Not that the captain had been given the chance.

I thought I would put myself forward just a little bit. 'What about our test, Alf?' I asked.

'What test, kid?'

'On the rules of soccer. You said a week ago we had to learn them by heart and then you'd give us a test.'

'And youse all learnt 'em, eh?'

'Yeah,' another chorus.

'No need for no test then, eh?' said Alf.

CHAPTER NINE

IN WHICH WE SET LOOSE OUR
TRUE ABILITY AND THEN GO
TO A PARTY

This was it! Moment of truth time.

The sun shone on a cold crisp day and there was poetry in my heart and soul.

We were to play at ten. When Lavender and I got there just after eight, Griller was ready and waiting. 'Jeez, mates, I thought youse was goin' ta be late. Been sweatin' it out proper. Been 'ere about an hour.' Griller sounded like Alf and looked like an outsize Lavender before she got into designer tracksuits and pink hair.

So hard to believe it was only six weeks since that first game of ours. So much water under the bridge and so many balls kicked since that far off day. This was it, now. This was it: true total soccer.

No waiting around for Ms Hennessey today. At nine on the dot the little white van smoked its way into view, Ms Hennessey at the wheel and Alf beside her with Persil draped over the back of his seat. No Mitch. Persil was chained so he couldn't escape.

Ms Hennessey and Alf took off for a warm-up jog around the ground. She was looking stunning in a rather nice navy-blue tracksuit. This didn't seem to please Lav, who was still wearing her old pink one. 'I don't really think that colour goes with Sharlene's flaming red hair,' said Lavender. She spoke rather sourly and softly as we all fell in line to jog round after the two of them.

'I don't know, sweetie. Woyal blue is weally wather nice on wed-heads,' said Maggie. 'Uncle Alfie bought it for her.'

Brown's Park First XI.

'Got new jerseys, eh?'

'Won't make no difference, eh?'

'We seen you last time when you was pink.'

'Even had a cat play for yer.'

'Played better'n all of yer too.'

'You all got murdered, eh?'

'Fifty-six nuthin', eh?'

I was on the point of replying to their friendly chat when Lav grabbed my arm. 'Don't stoop to their level, Tom. Discretion is always the better part of valour.'

'I'll do that little one for you, eh?' offered Griller.

'Over here!' roared Alf.

Soccer has always been about balance, quality and rhythm. It says so on my video tape. Well, that day we nearly had all three. Put more correctly, at times we had one but not the other two. At times we had two but not the missing third. And at times we had little bits of all three but not in very large quantities.

We also had spectators. Supporters. Mum, Dad and Mrs Poppy Gibson and Mr Lupescu, just returned from yet another successful railway engine and shotgun selling expedition over in Sydney-side. Griller's Mum turned up. I had never met the lady before, but there was a truly remarkable family likeness. Peter and Paula's Dad came along and used the opportunity to get to know quite a few neighbours, and became very friendly, very quickly with Mrs Poppy Gibson.

'Get up there. Get on that ball!' Alf.

'You on the right. Get there!' Alf.

'Mark that man. No! Not that one!' Alf.

'Lavender! Back him up. Get up there!' Alf.

'Good work, Paula.' Alf.

'No, woman. You're not allowed to kick it for them. They're not made of cottonwool, Shar.' Alf to Ms Hennessey.

'Kick him in the guts, Dwayney!' Mrs Spinks. 'Get him while he's down. Hammer the lights outa the little . . .' Lost on the wind. 'If you don't Dwayney, I will. That's my boy.' Mrs Spinks to Mrs Poppy Gibson.

'I can see that, darls. And that's my girl.' Mrs Poppy Gibson waved her thermos. 'The one with the pink hair.'

'A right cutey, eh?' Mrs Spinks.

Ten minutes in and the faces of Brown's Park were looking green as our new jerseys. They'd worn themselves out laughing at us before we even got started.

Heaven! True, true heaven. We timed our runs into the ball, like Alf said. We marked our men.

We kept possession if we got it, like Alf said. We matched each other's pace. A dream. An absolute dream.

A goal!!! A brilliant, brilliant goal, one the like of which I feel sure this ground had never seen. Near the end of the first half. Brown's Park, overcoming their absolute shock and surprise, were hammering hard. From in our half, pass, pass. Their forwards were knocking at our door. Whoosh . . . Right into the arms of Keeper Griller. Grill took one hard and evil look at the guy who'd kicked it. Then he looked at the ball. You could almost see the toss-up in Griller's mind as to which to put the boot into first.

'Kick it, Griller!' yelled Alf.

'Kick it, Dwayney,' yelled his Mum.

Griller made his choice. One long, low, hard and fast boot from one end of the field to the other. Past our defenders and their attackers. Past everyone and into orbit, and all eyes followed. It flew, flew, flew and fell. Wham! Right into the other goal.

The crowd went wild. Mrs Spinks grabbed Alf. Mrs Poppy Gibson grabbed Peter and Paula's Dad. My Mum grabbed my Dad. Griller ran this way and that, this way and that and then took one enormous jump into the arms of Ms Hennessey. Ms Hennessey, for all she was now fit as a lady buck rat, didn't quite have what it took to hold Griller and they fell into a tumbled jumble of arms and legs.

Half-time. 1–0 to us.

'Youse kids is goin' great guns,' said Alf.

Mrs Poppy Gibson and Mrs Spinks gave out food. 'Don't youse give 'em too much,' said Alf. 'Only half-way there and a long time to go yet.'

Over the other side of the field there was a huddle of Brown's Park. Sideways looks shot towards us. Then more huddled team talk and no time for them to eat.

Alf pepped us, 'Youse kids shocked the stuffin' outa them lot. Don't expect it to last,' he warned.

Alf was right.

A different Brown's Park fought back. They fought back hard. Disciplined and tough.

They scored.

They scored again.

Then they scored again.

Neat. Well planned and we weren't quick enough. We were tiring. Tiring very quickly.

They scored again. Griller, grim Griller, wasn't quick enough to cover the gaps. He moved out and they went in around him.

And then the magic moment. Lavender and me up front. Two-on-two against them. Don't know where Boggy had got to. One to the other. Kick. Volley. Kick. Timing. Perfect timing and almost, it seemed, a slow-motion play to the goal. And then . . . shoot! Their keeper jumped. He was too good, this one. But then one of his own sent it out across their goal line.

Corner. A classic. No slow-motion this time. Bog sent it in. To Lavender. To me. To her. Back to Boggy and then to me. Others in there now, in behind. Strike.

'GOAL!!!!'

Bliss. Absolute bliss. Hugs. A kiss, very quick, from Lav.

Who cared about the final score? 5–2 against us. This one, this time, had been a real, real game. A real victory. What a victory, for all we hadn't won. No one, but no one, could laugh at us this time. We had played a game, a real game, had done our best.

What a team! I was proud of every woman and man of them. My heart filled to bursting and, wonder of wonders, I hadn't even given a thought to the cops who might be after our jerseys.

'Well done, youse kids,' was all Alf said.

'Youse kids sure done us proud,' said Ms Hennessey. 'I knew you could do it.'

'Eh?' said Lav.

Mrs Spinks bashed everyone very hard on the back and all the others gathered in to give their congratulations. It was really sweet, that day. It was as sweet as if we'd won.

Well, maybe we had.

'Not the team I heard about,' the other coach said.

'Dunno what you heard, mate,' said Alf. 'Sure can't've been about this lot.'

'Dunno what things are coming to, girls in teams these days,' said the ref to Alf. 'Not on, as far as I'm concerned.'

'I know, mate. Nuthin we can do about it. Sign of the times, eh?' said Alf. 'There's three girls in this lot, ya know.'

'Must admit they're good little movers for all that,' said the ref. 'Little dark one over there. Centre-forward. Scored that last goal. She's a beaut. Great little mover, girlie,' he called.

He was pointing at me.

Mrs Poppy Gibson's engagement party was my first truly adult party. Although we of the team were only to be there until half-time, so to speak, it was still an event to look forward to. It might well be it was her engagement we were there for, but I felt sure she wouldn't mind us celebrating our victory at the same time. Mrs Poppy Gibson had a generous spirit.

There is no point asking me how a 5–2 loss can be called a victory. I know what I mean.

'For heaven's sake, Tommy, you've taken longer dressing than me. Get a move on,' said Mum.

'I think he's putting a pink rinse through his hair so as he won't feel out of it,' said Sue. She was also going to the party, with her new boyfriend, and to the Carlos Gibson branch of the festivities – but not until later on. Mum and Dad were coming to the Lavender Gibson segment so they could help with the catering.

'I should've learnt by now that when Florrie asks for just a wee hand with anything she really means body and soul,' said Mum, who had been catering all afternoon.

I think I really stunned them with my outfit.

'Uhh . . .' was all Mum said in a little gasping sort of choke.

'Ye gods!' said Dad.

'Not bad,' said Sue. 'You look like a cross between an undertaker and a magpie.'

Very clearly a success. Just as well. It had taken me hours. The dinner suit was a little on the large side but it's a true wonder what can be done with a needle and thread, a few safety pins and with my normal style and flair for fashion.

The pants were the hardest of all. I had to have the waist kind of round my chest otherwise the crutch came to my knees and it was hard to walk. As I would be dancing later on, this part of the engineering was quite important. It worked out all right because the jacket came well down below the knees, anyway. It draped beautifully, that jacket, and hid everything.

I am rather good with a needle and thread, even though I say so myself. We had a teacher once who insisted on teaching us all embroidery. Mum still has seven oven cloths hand-created by me in unusual ethnic designs. My training in embroidery had stood me in good stead because my new suit had fifty-five moth holes, and I embroidered little multi-coloured flowers and stars around each one with odd bits of wool. A truly stunning effect. It seems there's no end to my talents.

There was no way I could magic up a white shirt and bow-tie so I nicked an old white frilly blouse of Mum's and knotted a black shoelace round the neck and poked a red plastic rose through the knot. Couldn't quite make it with the black shoes, so I wore white sneakers to match the blouse and red socks to match the rose.

The fashionable wet look I wanted for my hair was achieved, cunningly I thought, by a fairly big dose of a rather nice bath oil that belonged to Mum.

'I'm not going anywhere with that,' said Sue.

'You don't have to, dear,' said Mum. 'You're off to see Carlos in the garage.' She looked at me in that way of hers. 'Come here,' she said. She gave me a very big hug and I felt my pants slipping down. 'I think you look . . . truly excellent,' she said and bent to kiss the back of my head. That's when she met up with her bath oil again.

The Gibson house was a riot of colour and a riot of noise. And it was still only eight o'clock.

'Say one thing for Florrie,' said Dad. 'When she gives a party she gives a party.' Which seemed a very obvious thing to say.

'Darlings! Darlings!! Darlings!!!' yelled Mrs Poppy Gibson. 'Thank God you're here. What on earth possessed me to invite Lavender's soccer team? I'll never know. The big one they call the Gorilla has been here since six and he's eaten all the canapes.'

Canapes are what the Mrs Poppy Gibsons of our world call little cracker biscuits with odds and ends on them. Didn't sound as if Griller had got really hungry yet or he'd have done for much more than just the canapes.

'And he's got a bottle of something hidden away somewhere and he's getting quite giggly, sweetie that he is.'

I sure hoped she had no coathooks handy. He always chuckled when he was hanging people, and it wouldn't be very nice if he started on Mrs Poppy Gibson's smaller-size guests.

The team were all there. All living it up, so to speak. There weren't very many adults yet. Only Mr and Mrs

Ng Ho Hanh, who ran the corner dairy. Mr Ng Ho Hanh is very small and I made a mental note to edge him well away from any coathooks and door handles when Griller lost control.

Lav and Maggie were together. 'It's gweat, pet. Weally, weally, gweat. The gweatest,' Maggie was shrieking. 'Bwing on the dancing men!'

'I'm here, doll,' I growled and the three of us danced together.

'Here. Put this in yer Coke,' Griller yelled to the three of us.

'Gwiller, you'll be the death of me,' screamed Maggie.

God knows, he could. I don't know what was in his bottle but the label on the outside said 'Paraffin.'

Lavender and I did a slow, hold-on-to-each-other, old-fashioned dance you don't often see these days. My heart lurched when she said, 'You look wonderful, Tommy.' Then she went on to say, 'Though, sadly, one day you'll have to grow up just like the rest of us. It'll be a sad day.' Then she caught her toe in one of my trouser cuffs, tripped and we both fell over.

We had a team bunny-hop which is one old-fashioned dance that's quite good. The house shook. It shook even more when the Carlos garage-guests came in to see what all the noise was and then joined in the old-time fun.

About nine, Alf and Ms Hennessey turned up. Still no Mitch? Mitch? Mitch who? Alf helped Mum serve our supper. Ms Hennessey looked an angel in a black, slinky, silk number with gold shoes. I stood by her. We made a truly stunning pair. 'Some outfit, Tommy,' she said. 'Flog it off your grandad, did you? Love the wee flowers.'

A woman of taste and substance, Ms Hennessey, whose days of bushman's shirts and blankets seemed to be over. So unlike Lavender Gibson, who was busy panting and puffing after Alf and looking like some small, pink whale. How could I have been so blind? Give her another half-hour and she'd be offering to make him pancakes.

We had a team toast from Alf. 'To youse kids. Best little soccer players I ever met, not that I ever met any before.'

Lavender jumped in with a reply. 'To dear Alf, our coach and friend-in-need-is-a-friend-indeed.'

Most of the team left about then. I didn't. First, Mum and Dad had to stay. After all, Mum was going to be Mrs Poppy Gibson's bridesmaid again. Second, I was supposed to be the partner of Lavender Gibson. Not that I wanted to be.

The rest of the party was quite dull and boring. The music got turned down so low it was drowned out by the Carlos Gibson branch of the party in the garage. However, one could see that Mrs Poppy Gibson had a great, great time. She truly enjoyed the company and conversation of Peter and Paula's father, and he seemed to very much enjoy hers. Peter and Paula's mother had a slight headache, which was a pity. The headache seemed to stop her enjoying herself and she dragged her husband away quite early on, which rather upset Mrs Poppy Gibson.

The future Mr Poppy Gibson was a dead loss. Too much basketball, most likely. Poor Eugene. He sat in a corner with a little smile on his dark ebony face and a sort of glazed look in his eye. I think it is possible that basketballers can catch a sort of punch drunkness and it seemed he had a touch of this. A bit like indoor sunstroke. When he spoke it was to say, 'Hey man!

Great stuff man. What a buzz.' A man of very few words, Eugene.

Alf and Ms Hennessey, very tired after their exciting day of soccer, just danced slowly, clinging to each other for support. Lavender tried to dance the same way with me, sort of copying the moves Ms Hennessey was making. 'Look at her. She's not the right woman for him,' she said several times. I don't quite know who wasn't the right woman for whom. Mrs Poppy Gibson for Eugene? Ms Hennessey for Alf?

For all we were now a thing of the past, dancing with Lavender Gibson was nice.

Mrs Lupescu danced with Dad. Mr Smith danced with Mum. Mrs Smith danced with Mr Ng Ho Hanh, even though he was a bit little to dance with. Mrs Smith sat on one of Eugene's knees for a rest. Mrs Poppy Gibson sat on his other knee and said, 'Isn't he just the cutest poppet? Who'd ever imagine this gorgeous hunk was out of Pocatello, Idaho?'

'What a buzz, man,' said Eugene.

Incredibly late, just after midnight, there was a new arrival. The Noise Control Officer from the Council, in answer to some complaints from neighbours of two streets away. Mrs Poppy Gibson gave him a drink, a kiss and the last two canapes. Alf went out to the garage to arrange for a bit less noise.

Just after this Mrs Spinks turned up. 'Where's my little Dwayney?'

'God knows, darling, and who cares? Here. Have a drink,' said Mrs Poppy Gibson. 'Wherever he is he can't be hungry.'

'Shoulda been home hours back. Hubby's worried sick.'

'For heaven's sake, Florrie, it's quite serious,' said Mum. 'You can't have children roaming the streets at this hour.'

First time in years anyone had said Griller was a child. And if he was roaming the streets it wouldn't be his safety I'd worry about.

'He's in the john.' It was Eugene who spoke, and in that one simple sentence doubled his conversation for the whole evening.

Leave him there, I thought to myself. Leave him there.

'Had to step over him and round him.' Eugene got right into it. 'Poor guy had flaked out. Stunned, man. I put him in the bath. What a buzz.'

Griller was there all right. Curled up and asleep in the bath. 'Leave him. Let him sleep, the wee pet,' said his mother. A wise decision, I thought. After making sure he was nice and comfy, Mrs Spinks joined the party and got the Noise Control Officer away from Mrs Lupescu for a dance. I didn't spot her finding the time to phone hubby to let him know all was well. Much later on the Noise Control Officer took her home in his Council car and she came back the next day to pick up Griller, who had slept for a long, long time.

The elderly continued to enjoy their fun and games for some time. They played a sort of musical chairs only they used knees instead of chairs. It seems to me there is little difference between their type of fun and our type of fun.

What a party!

What a day!

And what a night!

CHAPTER TEN

IN WHICH I AM HUMBLE IN
ALMOST-VICTORY

They say that any pack really needs a victim. Really needs that smell of blood. This is fully true of the student body of Greenhill Intermediate School. I think it's true of the staff, too.

There was none of that electric air as I, captain and leader of Greenhill Soccer Team C, stepped forward on the stage for the Monday sport assembly. 'Sadly,. fellow pupils and students, we suffered a slight loss. Despite a brave goal from our keeper, Dwayne Spinks, and a last-minute score by myself, I have to admit we let the school down by 5 to 2.' Yah, yah, yah. Stick it up your nostrils, I was saying to myself. I looked out on the sea of faces. You lot all wanted to hear 75–2, or better, 75–0.

Team A lost 6–1 and the Bs had a draw. No one at all could hoot at our effort.

'Well done, Don. Great effort. Great team of lads you've got there.' I didn't have the heart to tell him that ours was a unisexual team of sportspersons.

Things now gained what is called momentum. No more two-week gaps between games. We would have five in a row over the next month. Four nights a week with Alf and Ms Hennessey, except for Boggy who only had to turn out twice.

'You've heard the worst, I suppose,' said Lavender, miserably, on the bright, shining Monday morning.

'No. What?' Had Griller Spinks moved in for good?

'You must've.'

'Well, I haven't.'

'Blind and deaf to everything but your own concerns, Tommy. Selfish as ever. It's all round town. It's all round school.'

'Well, I haven't been in town and I come to school to work,' I said, rather stiffly. After all she hadn't even bothered to call me on Sunday to talk over Saturday, and Mrs Lupescu would only release Boggy for half an hour. She had offered me no refreshments and had gone back to bed with what she called 'the migraine to end all migraines.' I had offered her my good wishes, too, and the hope that Boggy's Mozart would soothe her poor head.

Lavender looked at me sadly with those deep blue eyes of hers, and I tossed up whether or not to let them pierce my heart yet again. 'Ms Hennessey has a new house-husband and it's Alf,' she said. 'She's moved into the Smith's granny flat.'

'Is that all? I knew that. Carlos told Sue,' I said.

Mrs Poppy Gibson's engagement party had worked miracles. Not only were Ms Hennessey and Alf a couple of lovebirds with their cat, Persil, in the Smith's back-yard, but Carlos and Sue had mended the break in their relationship, got rid of their previous lovers and spent all Sunday littering our sitting-room with their bodies, as well as leftover crisps and peanuts from the Gibson party. There were cartons of crisps left over because Eugene got truly vast quantities of them for free, on account of playing for the Johnson Potato Crisp Sub-

urbs United National League basketball team. I was
not all that keen on regaining Carlos as a possible future
brother-in-law, even if it could lead to meeting some
interesting step-in-laws in Pocatello, Idaho.

'You could've told me,' said Lav.

'I would've, if you'd come round. They did it on
Saturday after our game.'

'Did what?' asked Lavender.

'The big move.'

'Poor Mitch,' said Lav, softly and sadly. 'Poor, poor
Mitch. I quite liked him. Women can be fickle. Poor
Mitch.'

'Come off it, Lav. We didn't even know him. We
only saw him once.'

'Well, they've made their bed, now they've got to
lie on it,' said Lav.

'True,' I said. 'I think that's what they're doing.
Though Carlos tells me there are problems.'

'Are there?' Lavender brightened. 'What are they?'

'Everything I know is from Carlos. He is your
brother. Why don't you ask him?'

'Him? He's the ultimate sexist pig. I don't ask him
anything. You know that,' said Lavender. 'Now, tell
me, what are these problems?'

'It's poor old Persil. Seems it took to the Smiths' dog.'

'To their great dane? To Bonzo?'

'Yep. Belted old Bonzo good and proper. Carlos said
if he had his way he'd knock it on the head.'

'He couldn't,' said Lav. 'It's a lovely dog.'

'I think he meant Persil. Anyway, they can't get
Bonzo out from under the house and there's not much
room there. He's kind of stuck. Alf's going to have a
go today and Ms Hennessey has to keep Persil tied up.'

'Know it all, don't you?' said Lavender, bitterly and
sadly. 'Love! The curse of womankind, if you ask me.'

97

'You're not kidding,' I said, and meant every word of it.

Next day Lavender wore her new Presbyterian Ladies fur coat to school. While she still had her pink tracksuit on underneath it, I had a small and growing feeling that everything might be coming right although, clearly, I had missed out on the fur coat. Coming right? I sure hoped so. It had been a truly ill-wind blowing me no good. She also got back down to work on her first major literary assignment for the term: *My Life as the First Woman World Cup Soccer Star*, subtitled, *Move over Maradona; Make Way for Lavender Gibson*. I got to work on mine, too. Of a greater scientific interest, it will be called, *The Private Life of the Amoeba*.

Griller Spinks the hangman was one thing. Griller Spinks my new best mate was another matter.

'Come on, eh Tom. Nicked a packet of smokes from me old man. Let's go out the back. No one comes there.'

I had to take this bull by the horns, no matter what the serious and quite painful consequences could be. 'Grill,' I said. 'There's one thing you just got to know about me.'

'What's that, eh?'

'I am absolutely, adamantly and quite definitively against the consumption of tobacco,' I said firmly.

'Wha?' said Grill.

'I don't smoke,' I said.

'So what. I'll have one, then.' And he did.

'And I must caution you, Dwayne. Smoking endangers health irreparably. The government and other scientific experts all say so.'

'Wha?'

This was one big problem. 'Look, Grill. Don't do it. Not now you are big in sport. It's no good for you

98

and with your big success in soccer it's not right. You must set an example to the little kids, because they will look up to you.' Or down on him depending upon whether they were hanging from coathooks or not. 'You don't need to smoke. It'll rot your lungs out, and Alf doesn't smoke.'

'Don't he?'

'Nup. He's never smoked in his life. Not ever.'

I had no idea about this but it did seem I was on the right track. 'Alf says if he ever catches any of us, and he'll sure know, we'll wish we had never been born and we won't ever sit down again.'

'Wow!' said Griller and tossed his lighted cigarette and the whole pack into a rubbish bin. 'Wow!' Then he cheered up a lot. 'Seen that little new kid in Room 18, eh? Seen him round? Come on. Let's go and do him. He's so small even you could lift him, eh. Should squawk real good. You get him round the back, then I'll grab 'im.' He smiled sweetly.

I shuddered. I couldn't be expected to stand by and enjoy human sacrifice. Could I?

'Look, Grill. We'll go and find Lav and Maggie. Lav's got something you'd really like to see. It's real great.'

'I bet,' he grinned.

'She's got her new coat. Gee, you should see it. It's real rabbit fur. Well, some of it is, just here and there. It sure is great.'

It worked. This time. Probably there was a limit and I guessed one day I'd have to see a bit of blood spilt along the path of improving Griller Spinks' intentions and attitudes. Rome wasn't built in a day, and neither was Griller. There was no way I could win this one by myself, and Lavender, Maggie, Bog and the others were just going to have to play a part. Who was to tell if, like Boggy, Grill might have a truly great interest in

99

the work and music of Mozart? Mind you, Boggy's close family connections with Count Dracula might be nearer Griller's tastes.

It was while we were all sitting together and Grill was trying on Lavender's fur coat that the full taste of our sweet sporting success hit home. Three, four guys in a group came up to us. Only two short weeks ago this lot had been well in with the jeerers. They had been those who laughed loudest. One was even in Team A.

'Had a good game, eh, Saturday?' said one.

'Pretty tough, that Brown's Park team.'

'Jeez, you got some coach, that Smith guy.'

'Any chance of us gettin' a game, eh?'

'Them girls in your team. Could dump 'em. Use us. Let us in.'

'Piss off,' said Griller. 'You wanna coathook up ya back, eh?'

They slunk off in a very quick slink. Sure had his uses, did Griller.

'Thank you, Gwiller. You're a weal gentleman,' said Maggie.

Which was stretching it just a bit. 'Yeah,' said Griller. 'Gizza go yer coat, eh Lav.'

She took it off and gave it to him. 'I think it suits you, Griller,' she said.

'Poor little bunny rabbits, eh,' said Griller, stroking a little patch of fur. 'Fancy doin' in them little bunny rabbits just to make an old coat. Real cruel, eh?'

They say we all have unexpected sides to our natures. Who would ever have guessed that Griller Dwayne Spinks, Top Torturer of Greenhill Intermediate, could have a tear sliding down his cheek at the thought of some long, long, long dead rabbits? 'Suits you, Grill,'

I said. 'You look like an Eskimo.' I thought I might cheer him up.

'Gwiller, I must say that all of our soccer is having a wonderful effect on your fuller figure,' said Maggie.

I suppose this was true of all of us. None of us had ever exercised this way before. Never. What we had found sheer agony two weeks ago we now took for granted. We even impressed Alf. 'Youse kids! Another season of this and I'll have youse all in league or Aussie rules.'

It was at our first practice before our third game that I realised the Eternal Triangle had not quite been squashed flat. Between fitness and skills practice, Lavender made her challenge. It was just Alf and the team. Ms Hennessey was home cooking Alf's dinner.

'I wonder, Alf,' she started, 'if perhaps we have made quite the right choice for leader of our team. I wouldn't like to mention any names or personalities, if you see what I mean.'

If he couldn't, I could. After all, there was only one name to mention. Mine!

'Can't say I do, dearie,' said Alf.

'I do feel,' continued Lavender, 'that one's captain should be a dominant and self-assertive leader, with a bit more personality than our one's been blessed with.'

The traitor! The cunning little serpent and traitor.

'Oh, yeah,' said Alf. 'Go on.'

'One leads by example, it's often said,' said Lavender Gibson. 'And far be it from me to complain, but in all honesty I think I would be the better man, person I mean, for the job. And Maggie says so, too.'

'I never said anything, Uncle Alfie.' Maggie got in very quick and Lav shot her down with one glance. 'Honest I didn't.' Maggie closed her eyes.

101

'Look, kid,' said Alf to Lavender. 'Youse lot've had two games. So far they killed youse in the first one and while 5–2 sure ain't cooked chook, it ain't toppa the dung heap either. Geddit?'

'I like Tom,' said Grill.

Why was it that so often when Griller spoke it struck terror deep into my heart?

'Tom's okay by me,' said Boggy. 'Siddown, Lav.' He tried an Alf-like roar.

'And I never said anything, Uncle Alfie. Weally I didn't,' said Maggie.

'Whaddabout youse others, then?'

Youse others, dear souls, gave a full vote of confidence in my leadership.

Lavender took her defeat like any good man or woman. 'You mustn't take it personally, Tommy. It was all for the good of the team. You do understand that, Tom?' she said to me as we walked home.

'Oh, yeah?'

'Of course it was. And you must've noticed I made a big point of not mentioning names or personalities,' she said.

'You didn't have to, Lav,' I said.

'No hard feelings, Tom-tit?' She smiled shyly down at me in that way she has that can truly wring my heart.

'Course not, Lav. Now you can shout me a milk-shake to make up for it.' Cute little traitor that she was.

'We'll have to call at the boutique. I'm broke,' said Lav. 'There is just a teensy wee lesson for you some-where in there, Tommy.'

'What? At the boutique?'

'No, dummy. In my leadership challenge.'

'Yeah,' I said. 'I reckon it's something about watching

that place between my shoulder blades when my best mates get out their knives.' I said it very nicely.

'It's my opinion, Tom,' she said, 'for what it's worth, and it's worth quite a lot, that you must be more dominant. It's not good enough to just be a strong leader; one must be seen to be a strong leader as well.'

Mrs Poppy Gibson was out. Carlos sat in the accessory bar getting it off with his mother's part-time junior shop assistant. It seemed to me that this guy's personal habits could only be described as the essence of evil and ten times as bad as Ms Hennessey's tomcat, Persil. If only my poor sister Sue could see her idol now.

'Where's Mum?' said Lav.

'Out,' said Carlos. 'Bug off.'

'Where?' said Lav.

'Parade of new spring things in the city,' said the assistant.

'Hoppit,' said Carlos.

'I want five bucks,' said Lavender. 'I need two new exercise books and a protractor for school. I'll get it out of the till.'

'Mum said you wasn't to touch the till,' said Carlos. 'Now, get.'

'What Mother said, Carlos, dear, was that you were not allowed to touch the till, and for very good reasons, only half of which Mummy knows about . . . so far,' said Lavender, and I could see in these few, short and well chosen words of hers exactly what she meant by dominant personality.

'Here,' said the assistant. 'Take the five and I'll tell your Mum.'

'Now bug off,' said Carlos.

'Up yours,' said Lavender.

'Sue says she'll see you later, Carlos. Round at your place tonight,' I said. 'And if you want her to bring your underwear you left at our house on Sunday just to give her a ring,' I lied. 'She's washed and ironed it all for you.'

I won't stoop so low as to outline Carlos' reply or describe the physical actions he said he would perform on my person if he caught me. I got out the front door of the boutique just before Mrs Poppy Gibson walked in and got knocked over by her son.

Lavender says it's all because of his Portuguese blood.

'What do you know about dominant personalities, Dad?' I asked that night, and settled down for a father–son deep and meaningful chat.

'Could write a book on it, Tom,' he said. 'Let's face it. I live with three of them.'

'I need to know. Seriously.' I looked at him.

'I am serious,' he said. 'Look,' he held out his hands and made them shake. 'See what it's done to me. Physical wreck. Changed an ordinary nice middle-aged bloke into what I am today.'

'I have a problem,' I said.

'Don't we all,' said Dad.

I worry, sometimes, about the man's unserious attitude to life and all it means. 'It would appear that I am not dominant enough. I am not assertive enough and I am a big failure at leadership.'

'Lavender been on at you again, Tom? Is that it?' said Dad. 'God knows, it's about time Florrie kept a closer eye on that kid. She's a right menace. Carlos is sure a credit to her but that girl . . . Whew!'

Which all shows just how little one can trust the judgement of your older generation. 'I am not here to talk about Lavender and Carlos Gibson,' I said.

'Have it your own way,' said Dad. 'So, you're worried about leadership, dominance and assertiveness?' He did get serious. 'Okay. First off, why on earth do you need, does anyone need, to dominate others? Tell me that. Seems to me it's only another name for bullying. You're not a bully and you never will be, thank God. You may well be many other undesirable things but you're not a bully. Leadership?' He smiled. 'Silly little twerp. I'm so damn proud of what you do and what you've done . . .' He smiled again. 'You're okay.'

'Uh?'

He went on smiling like a grinning cat. 'Look. You've got together a most unlikely bunch of your friends and mates and you've taken on the establishment. Good heavens, kid, don't talk to me about leadership!'

I had not the slightest idea what he was talking about. 'Have I?'

'In no time flat you've got your soccer team up and going from nothing at all. All the unsporting or non-sporting deadbeats no one ever gave a chance to before. No one was ever going to give them a chance, either. All right, so there's been a spot of luck in people you've attracted along the way. Your Ms Hennessey and poor old Alf Smith. Dammit, no one could say you lack enthusiasm or leadership. Come to think of it, you probably *are* a dominant personality or whatever you call it. Exactly like your mother.' He looked up as she walked in.

'Just like his mother what?' Mum asked.

'Oh, charming, sincere, hardworking. All those things like that,' he grinned.

'Yeah, and what do you want? Both of you?'

'I'd very much like a cup of cocoa, please Mother.' No sense in not making the most of every opportunity. They don't come all that often.

'You know where the kitchen is, sweetheart. Sue and Carlos are out there and would probably like one, too. Such a lovely boy,' said Mum.

They were all blind. 'Reckon I'll give it a miss for a while, Mum.'

'Have I answered your question?' asked Dad.

'What question?' asked Mum.

'Just between us two men,' said Dad.

'Oh. That sort of question,' said Mum. 'Man talk.'

'That's sexist, Mother. Had you been here you would have been quite welcome to join in,' I said.

'As it was, I was finishing ironing ten soccer uniforms and just about the largest sweatshirt ever made. And that, young man, is truly sexist. I'm glad it's only once in the season I have to do it. Would have been there until tomorrow if Carlos hadn't given me a hand. Not all of you males are sexist, I'm glad to see.'

Good old Carlos! I hoped she hadn't given him mine to do.

'All right on what we were talking about?' asked Dad.

'Yep. I reckon,' I said. 'Thanks.'

'You're welcome.'

Sometimes this older guy can be quite sensitive to the needs of his son. Truly surprising, my father.

CHAPTER ELEVEN

IN WHICH CULTURE REARS ITS HEAD

Game three. St Joseph's B.

Knocking at the door in a two-all draw.

According to Alf we should have won. 'Youse kids've gotta assert yourselves.'

'It's in the leadership, Alf,' said Lavender, who never gave up.

'I thought we were quite assertive enough, Alf,' I said. 'After all, Boggy did get sent off.'

The heat of the moment, near the end of the game and after we had equalised and then almost scored again. Boggy bit his opponent after the opponent had kicked Boggy. I'm sure my face drained of all blood and I did my best to keep a close eye on the bitten one to make sure his didn't, too. Would a tetanus shot be enough after a bite from one of this family?

Our fame had spread. Among the spectators were Mum and Dad, Mrs Poppy Gibson and Eugene, Carlos Gibson and Sue, Mrs Spinks, Mr and Mrs Lupescu, Mrs Smith but not Mr Smith, who had put his back out digging Bonzo the great dane out from under their house. A very small man, possibly Mr Spinks, Peter and Paula's mother but not their father, and Wilson's three sisters who are triplets and one of our local well-known sights because they all look the same. Quite a few others were unknown to me and were likely the family connections of Brian, Nick and Gordon. And, great wonder of great wonders, our kindly old Mr Harvey, principal of Greenhill Intermediate and truly a gentleman. An even truer gentleman may well have come to lend a hand and help out before we were struck by fame. Still, better late than never, as they say.

Naturally Alf, Ms Hennessey and Persil were there and at the ready. Persil was chained to what was left of the front bumper of Ms Hennessey's little white van because the back was being used for morning tea refreshments. Clearly our games were turning into quite a social drawcard and it was now necessary for all the parents to bring a plate of morning tea. Mrs Poppy Gibson had brought a cask of wine and the older spectators were having quite a good time, even Mr Harvey.

Eugene brought his North American style and flair and between glasses of wine led our cheer team: 'Ra ra ra, one two three, Greenhill C, the team for me.' His future wife got quite excited and rather carried away as cheerleader, and I overheard Mum say to her at one stage, 'Tone it down, Flo, for godsake. You're not in Idaho yet.'

Alf had his hands full. Apart from directing us he also had to control the audience, and at half-time he didn't have a chance to pep talk us because he had to give the oldies a lecture.

'It's a kids' game and the little sods is givin' it heaps, but youse lot can stop yellin' at them.' Mainly to Mrs Spinks. 'Youse can call out "well done" if youse want to, but do it to both lots, see. Not just our ones.'

I thought this was a bit unfair. After all, the spectators on the other side of the field were yelling only for their team.

'And don't you be sayin' to your Dwayne you'll up him with yer brolly, Mrs Spinks, please. He's doin' a great job jumpin' up and down in that goal.'

'You can't kill whatever kid knocked down your Paula,' he said to Paula's Mum. 'She's a goer, that one, even if she's little. Youse lot see 'er flatten that big bloke before?'

'And I'm surprised at you, too, Mr Harvey . . .' said Alf.

I never found out why, because Mrs Spinks, Mrs Poppy Gibson, Eugene, Carlos, Sue and most of the others started up again, 'Ra ra ra, one two three, Greenhill C, the team for me.'

During the second half a couple of cops cruised by, stopped and joined Ms Hennessey.

The jerseys? Dear God, not our jerseys. Not that.

Afterwards, when there was no one around, I asked her why they stopped and what they wanted. 'A cup of coffee, Tom. Why?'

'Just wondered.' A cup of coffee? More to this than met the eye. Just the way they worked, these guys.

'Besides, one of them is my cousin,' said Ms Hennessey. 'A sort of family visit, you might say.'

I had heard that one before.

'Life's full of surprising turns,' I said to Lavender Gibson as we cruised the streets of our suburb on our bicycles later that same day.

'What d'you mean?' she yelled at me as we negotiated another tricky corner just in front of an insane motorist who sat on his horn right behind us. 'And get out of the way of that madman. He'll do for you.'

'Two bicycles are entitled to as much room as one car,' I yelled back. 'We've got four wheels, too. We've got our rights.'

'He's going to squash your rights unless you move over,' said Lavender. 'And traffic statistics have no rights at all.'

The old guy in the car did a whole lot of obscene finger signs as he drove past us. I pretended not to see. Some people are best treated with absolute ignore.

'Greenhill is certainly a superb suburb of our fine city,' I said when we were at last at rest on the steps of the branch library. 'Friendly, homely and welcoming to every stranger.'

'You're twisted,' said Lav. 'You've always reckoned it was the pits, same as me. One good thing about Eugene is at least I'll get to see Idaho and the wider world we hear so much about. Sooner than you, too, unless you come for a vacation, as we call it.'

'Stuff Idaho. This is my patch, my home,' I said.

'I don't believe I'm hearing the same man, the same person I mean, who used to reckon that when God created the world in his own image he made Greenhill the . . .'

I broke in quickly. 'I think I've matured in my thinking since that far-off day, Lav,' I said.

'Yeah. Tell that to the birds. It was only about last month you said it. Tommy, it's all since you got into big-time soccer and all your leadership potential spilled out. Don't get all carried away. We haven't won a game yet.'

'We're knocking at the door, Lav. I feel it,' I said.

'Yeah, well, these steps are freezing my bum off even through my furs,' said Lavender. 'Let's move it.'

There was no fur on the rear-side of her coat but I thought I wouldn't mention it. 'Let's call on Ms Hennessey and Alf. They'd love to see us and might give us a drink. If not, Maggie will.'

'Yeah,' said Lav, with some enthusiasm. 'We might see Persil beat up the great dane.' Under the skin she was as bad as her brother Carlos.

'After that I've got to call on Mrs Lupescu.'

'I'm not going there,' said Lav. 'Why do you have to go?'

Mrs Lupescu did not exactly go for Lavender in a big way, and I guess, in some ways, Lav is an acquired taste. 'Poppy's peculiar little girl,' she had been know to say, and more than once. In fact quite often. 'Gives me the shivers. So intense, and nothing like her mother.'

'I want to check on Boggy. Only two weeks to go till the debut. Boy, that'll sure be some day,' I said. It sure would be some day. The last game in our first round and against that team of teams, Greenhill A.

We knocked and knocked on the door of the granny flat, but no one answered. 'They must be out,' Lav said to Maggie.

'Weally,' said Maggie. 'They were there five minutes ago, I'm sure. Come on in. I'm just making Gwiller and me a cup of coffee. He came round to check on poor Bonzo. That dweadful cat'll have to go. Mummy says it's making Bonzo all neuwotic, and all Uncle Alfie does is laugh.'

'Yeah,' said Griller. 'My guinea pig gets like that when me Mum's pet magpie pecks 'is cage.'

We finished our coffee, and all had a chat with Bonzo, who was back under the house. Well, Griller had the chat because no one else could fit in the trapdoor with him.

'I just thought I'd come and check on Bogdan, Mrs Lupescu,' I said. 'I don't want you to think soccer is the only thing on my mind.'

'I've never thought that, Tom,' she said.

'I still have time for the finer and higher things of life.' Lay it on thick. It always helps, or so I've found, with the Mrs Lupescus of this world.

'I'm glad to hear it, Tom. You'd better come in,' said Mrs Lupescu. While she didn't sound one hundred per cent welcoming, the indications weren't too bad.

'How's Mr Lupescu?' I asked politely.

'He's quite well,' she said.

'Shotguns and trains selling okay, then?' Older people truly appreciate kids who don't dry up after just saying hello.

'What?' said Mrs Lupescu.

Boggy came in and we settled down to a good chat about his upcoming debut. There's nothing like a bit of culture to get us all going.

'It's only the third movement that needs anything done,' he said. 'Apart from that I reckon it's all in place.'

'Bet Mozart didn't have any trouble, even with the third movement,' I said, keeping my voice low because Mrs Lupescu sure had good hearing.

'Well, he wouldn't, would he? He wrote the stupid thing,' said Bog.

'Yeah. And he was younger than you, too, Bog,' I rubbed it in. It was my true wish that Boggy wouldn't get a big head about his excellence. 'I think that guy Mozart must have thought in music. You know how we think in words and pictures in the mind? For example, I see Lavender. Then I sound the name 'Lavender' as a word: L-A-V-E-N-D-E-R.'

'You smell Lavender,' said Boggy.

'Don't get smart with me, Bog. You know what I mean. Mozart, now, he wouldn't have done that,' I said.

'Well, he never knew Lavender, did he? He was dead well before Lavender's time,' said Bog. 'Lucky Mozart, eh?'

'But if he had known her . . .' At times Boggy could miss not only the point of an argument but the whole argument itself. 'If he had known Lavender he would not have seen her as a picture . . .'

'Well, she's not much of one.'

Ignore! 'Nor as a series of letters. I reckon your mate, Mozart, would have seen Lavender in his mind as a whole series of little black and white piano notes.' I hummed an example for him. 'Get what I mean? That little tune could actually say Lavender. Get it?'

'Not really,' said Bog. 'But then I often don't get what you mean, so don't worry.'

'You've a nice voice, Tom,' said Mrs Lupescu, returning to the room with a tray of refreshments. 'Would you care to stay for dinner? We're not having much but you'd be most welcome.'

I bet there'd be good red meat somewhere on the menu. Very rare steak most likely. 'I'd really like that, Mrs Lupescu. I'll have to ring Mum.'

'It's all right, dear. I'll do it. Must check on how many seats she wants me to get for the concert, anyway.'

Everyone, naturally, of our wider acquaintance, was going to the concert. If you ask me it's just a cunning trick on the part of the authorities to fill up the seats of a concert hall. Put on any kid, and if they've got enough friends and relations to fill the place, you're home and hosed even if the kid isn't any good at all.

Not that Boggy was bad. Quite, quite truthfully he was brilliant. My Mum said so. Not quite thirteen and he already had nearly all the skills, techniques and tricks he'd ever need for a lifetime job in piano playing. Or so Mum said. Apart from anything else he'd sure make big bucks and was well worth keeping in with for this alone. All he needed now, according to Mum, was heart, soul, spirit, guts and determination. She should know.

She once played the piano herself before turning into a lawyer.

Boggy. A very good friend and a fine piano player. Lavender reckons he's not commercial and there's a limited market for Mozart. Well, maybe what he does isn't much like heavy metal, but I'd always go along and see him. Not see him, really. Hear him, actually, because Bog sure isn't much to look at for hours on end. There's only five per cent more of him than there is of me. We worked it out one day.

Boggy's concert gets to go on television, and I'm hoping against hope that the cameras can leave him alone long enough for a quick shot or two of the audience. I do intend dressing for the occasion.

We had lasagne for dinner. Lasagne and salad. It's a very popular dish in our suburb. I can't think why, except that minced beef is often on special at our supermarket and is sort of cheap as meat goes. Not anywhere near as delicious as your good old rare steak. Mr and Mrs Lupescu had a glass or two of red wine. Or least that's what they said it was.

CHAPTER TWELVE

IN WHICH WE REAP OUR REWARD AND SO DOES BOGDAN

We came undone! Disaster! Shame! Blame! Ker-Boom!!!

Against St Pius X. For interested readers, St Pius X was an old Catholic leader and Pope of the previous century who gave his name to a lot of schools and was made a saint. I looked him up in the Encyclopedia Britannica as a matter of interest, and he gets a good write-up. It said he also modernised Catholic churches. A pity he hadn't got round to the one near us; it's still a truly old-fashioned building.

More to the point of this story, he gave his name to a lot of very tough schools, probably in the hope that his saintly and heavenly ways might rub off on all the animals who went to them. Nothing at all saintly or heavenly had rubbed off on this lot.

Their team had several Griller Spinks lookalikes, and of all the rest, there wasn't one who was smaller than Lavender. And that means quite big.

6–0. 6–0! It might be better than 32–0, but not much. Let me tell you, it feels much the same.

'How the mighty have fallen,' I heard Mr Crow mutter and chuckle cruelly to Mr White as I stood on the stage at assembly.

'Well done, Don,' said Mr Harvey.

I didn't believe his kind words of comfort. After all he was now more or less a permanent member of our supporters' club, so he could be said to be on our side. He had struck up quite a close friendship with Mrs Poppy Gibson and I think she was beginning to look upon him as the father she had never had. He sure enjoyed his glass of wine, did Mr Harvey.

We took some flak and there were no applicants, this week, who wanted to come over to our side. Dear Alf was as understanding as ever. 'They was hard little sods and youse lot did as good as yer could. Winning isn't everything, though God knows, I'd like youse all to chalk up one. Must 'ave another word with yer Mums and Dads. Not the usual gotta supporters far as I can see. Gotta tone it down. Takes yer mind off of it.'

He was right on that count.

We now had pre-match snacks, half-time snacks, and after-match lunch. The food was excellent. When no one was looking Griller got into Mrs Poppy Gibson's wine cask, and that hadn't helped our second half.

Eugene's cheerleaders had expanded, and a good number of ladies who were friends of his or friends of Carlos Gibson, or were queueing up to be future friends of one or the other, had heard where the Saturday action was to be had, and turned up to join in. It took up a lot of Mrs Poppy Gibson's time just controlling their enthusiasm, and she didn't look too happy until Mrs Spinks gave her a hand with her umbrella.

Ms Hennessey didn't let us off as lightly as Alf. 'He thinks the world of you kids and what you've done,' she said.

'What Alf's done,' said Lav.

'No. Alf doesn't see it that way at all. He's worked his butt off helping you all, but you've had to do the

116

work. Not one of you has fallen by the way, so to speak. Not one of you has even missed a day of school since all this started.'

'I know,' said Griller with some feeling. It was the longest straight stretch he'd ever done without an odd day or two off.

'Not one of you has missed a practice,' said Ms Hennessey. 'So don't you think I'm criticising.'

Then she settled down to a good old criticising. 'I do think the whole thing has gone to your heads. Just you think about what Alf said to you last night. You still haven't won a game, you know.'

'Alf said winning's not important, Ms Hennessey,' I said.

'And he's right,' said Ms Hennessey. 'You know me. I couldn't care less if you lost 32–0 every time, if that was the best you could do. I'm not exactly into winning. You should know that.' And she smiled. 'Me? With my interest in sport?' She laughed. 'What I'm saying, pets, is you get in there and win a game. At your best you are quite capable of winning one. And I'm going to have a word with one or two of your supporters as well. If I'm asking you to play the game, well, they must come to the party, too.' She laughed again. 'Wrong choice of words, I think. Still, you know what I'm getting at.'

The new, serious Ms Hennessey could still have her little joke, bless her.

'How's Persil?' asked Griller, sadly.

'Persil? Well, Persil's gone to a better home, a better place,' she said.

Griller, newly fit, boomed out, 'You didn't let Carlos Gibson do him, did ya?'

'Don't be silly, Dwayne. Of course not. It's just that Persil didn't get on too well with Maggie's dog. He's gone home to my mother for a while. Besides, Carlos couldn't, wouldn't harm a hair on the head of anything.'

How did Carlos Gibson, psycho that he was, get away with it?

Griller settled and then thought for a while. 'Jeez! You really got a mother, then?'

Back to the drawing-board. Well, back to the gym and the far field, even if it was freezing cold and wet all that week. Except for Boggy, who had got the whole week off from practice and three days off from school. In my next life I fully intend coming back as a piano player.

June dragged into July, colder, wetter. Just our typical southern hemisphere, Antarctic-type winter. To make matters worse I was having heavy trouble with *The Private Life of the Amoeba*. There appears to be very little to write about these wee single-cell creatures, and they simply do not have a private life of any great interest to anyone but themselves.

Mrs Poppy Gibson gave us a night out. An all-American dinner at a Pizza Hut, sampling one of the great national dishes of the North American people. Pretty good, too. Lavender and me, Carlos and Sue and Mrs Poppy Gibson of course. The highlight was to be watching Eugene and the rest of the Johnson Potato Crisp Suburbs United National League basketball team beat the hell out of the Black and White Cartage and Longhaul All-Saints, another big league team.

What would this nation do, basketball-wise, without the help of our dear cousins, the North Americans? It seemed that most of those on the stadium court that night were either American Blacks or American Whites. And there was even one American Indian, or so the programme said. I must say he looked most unlike the

118

North American Ethnics we see on our television screens. Unless I had spotted the wrong one. Anyway, it is certainly great that so many of them thought to come all the way over here to play for our enjoyment and help us out.

Basketball is a great consumer sport and we worked our way through a lot of the foods that were available to consume. Mrs Poppy Gibson is always one generous lady with her favours and hospitality.

It was quickly clear that the future Mr Poppy Gibson was one big star. A very big expert at the slam-dunk, and master of the court. He was a joy to see in action. Truly a very elastic Black in his wondrous ducking, dancing and diving, he was a real inspiration to us all, and I spotted one or two tricks I could well put to use in our upcoming game against Greenhill Intermediate Team A. It is true to say that basketball is a somewhat different sport but it is my experience that many of the principles and tactics are the same regardless of the game. Except, that is, for synchronised swimming which Lav and I took up last summer down at the Municipal Baths. A truly strange sport. They had it in the last Olympics and only eleven people turned up to see it. We were doing quite well down at the baths and we sure had more than eleven watching us, when one of the attendants tossed us out. He reckoned, quite wrongly, that we were a menace to everyone else in the pool and that if we wanted to practise drowning we could do it just as well at home in the bath.

Eugene dominated the game, although from time to time he had to have a sit-down for very minor breaking of the rules. I could tell he really appreciated the rests. Naturally we encouraged him as much as we could. After all, he was just about one of the family.

'For God's sake, lady. Shut those damn kids up and

keep them still,' said one very rude man sitting just by us.

I tried to explain to him, politely of course, that we were here in order to support our brother, Eugene, number 34 for Johnson's, and clearly the star of the game. At which the rude guy looked very strangely at Mrs Poppy Gibson and said something to her I couldn't quite catch. She hit him with her rolled-up copy of the evening paper, which she had brought to read when her Eugene was not in action. Mrs Poppy Gibson is not your natural good sport and only takes an interest when Eugene, Carlos or Lavender are actively involved.

In the end the Potato Crisps beat the Longhaul All-Saints by 98–97 in the final five seconds, and all due to Eugene's great skill and cunning play. Half the audience cheered and the other half booed, and there was much talk around us of being robbed, and that Eugene should be deported on the next plane north. Mrs Poppy Gibson went properly wild at this, and then we all went home to her place for coffee and pumpkin pie.

It is truly startling how electric this elastic North American Black, from Pocatello, Idaho, can be on the basketball court, and what a dead drag he can be in a social setting. No matter how hard I tried to engage him in sport talk on the finer points of his game, and how he might pep it up just a little bit here and there, all I could get from him was, 'Un huh, huh er man. Right on, kid,' or something similar.

I can't for the life of me think what Mrs Poppy Gibson sees in him.

What can I say? Readers, I will not keep you in suspense because that's where I know you are.

We thrashed, truly thrashed Greenhill Intermediate Team A! We thrashed, truly thrashed our sporting cousins 1–0. It may well be the greatest highpoint in my life to date, except, that is, for the exact moment of my birth when I first set eyes upon this great world.

We were brilliant, even if I say so myself. True poetry in action. I have, in fact, penned a few lines of blank verse to mark the occasion. When, days later, I gave a copy of it to Ms Hennessey, she promised to sleep with it under her pillow. Clearly, she was deeply affected. Here it is:

Play the ball
Play the man
Play the game.
Soccer, dear soccer, how we adore thee
And sing thy praises all the more. See!

Then the truly clever bit;

This was not a grudge match,
If they will not budge, catch
The ball on toe and run
Fast into the setting sun.
We bless the day when it was seen
Us lot wasted Greenhill A team.

And, because it is blank verse, just a simple final line,

1–0 YAH!!!!!!!!!!!

The eleven exclamation marks are, of course, symbolic. The setting sun bit is not quite right. We played in the middle of the morning. All poets reading this will know that you are allowed to do this sort of thing in poetry. Poetry doesn't have to be exactly, fully truthful, providing the message is clear. My message, I know, is quite clear.

Even the ref admitted to being quite astonished at our monstrous success. I heard him talk to Mr Crow at half-time. 'Your lot should be slaughtering them, Crow. Ball's in their half most of the time. Most of them look scared stiff to kick it at the goal. What's wrong with them?'

'If you had to face that goalie, mate, you'd be too scared to kick it at him, too,' said Mr Crow. It confirmed what I had always known. Mr Crow was not a good sport. Still, it was nice that he had, at last, come to see us play.

Indeed, half of our school's staff seemed to be there. Mr Harvey, of course, now one of our keenest supporters, and increasingly a good friend of Mrs Poppy Gibson. Mr Crow, Mr White, Ms Hennessey, naturally. And there, too, bless her, dear old Miss Webster, my very own teacher.

'It was easier to come, Thomas, and see for myself than put up with listening again to a blow by blow, ball by ball account from you, for the whole of next week.'

Truly bless her. I bet I get a good report at the end of the term.

Half-time and we were evenly poised at 0–0.

Our supporters' club were all there but they'd had training talks from both Alf and Ms Hennessey. 'Too much squawkin' this time and I'll boot the lotta youse out,' he said. Alf always had the right word for the right occasion. 'Youse lot support their A Team, too. All the same school, yer know.' Dear old Alf. Sometimes he could carry things too far.

The A Team had their gang of supporters, too. They were on the other side of the field from our lot, and there was quite a bit of heated and vicious slanging going on, mainly from their side, of course. Alf went over and had a few quiet chats with them and things quietened down a bit.

Alf knew how much this game meant to us. 'I done me best, kids. Youse all know that.' He turned to Ms Hennessey. 'It'll be a bloody miracle, Shar.' And he whispered something softly to her about silk purses. I must let him know he can buy one for her at the Poppy G. Boutique and Accessory Bar.

As is my habit, I must be absolutely honest. We were slightly outplayed. Only twice in the first half did we manage to get the ball into their half. Both of these times were when Griller got tired of all the bees buzzing around the honey-pot of our goal and really stuck his boot into it.

The second half looked just about as tight. Every time we had a go at getting through we seemed to get penalised. I have a suspicion that the ref was a close friend of Mr Crow, but I must not accuse him of being unfair. Admittedly Lav did get a bit rough now and again, which was understandable. She's never liked her opponent, and this showed just a tiny bit in the way she played.

'Come on, Greenhill. Get into it!' Hard to say which team they meant.

'Liven it up a bit, kids.'

'Kick 'im in the guts, Dwayney.' You could never keep a good Mrs Spinks down.

'Don't let that big ape frighten the lights outta ya!'

'Get up there. Pass. Pass. Get in. Get it in. Come on! Shoot!'

It wasn't working. Not for us. We were so hemmed in we couldn't get out. Out. Throw in. Out. Corner. Penalty. Miss. Penalty. Miss.

Never in all his life had Griller worked so hard. He was excellent. Brilliant. Even if the A Team were not exactly keen on kicking at his goal, there did come times when they just had to. Not once did he let the ball through. There was a grim, grim look in his eye, but not once, either, did he let go with his temper and have a go at the buzzing flies. Good old Grill. Excellent sportsperson.

The miracle happened. I had started to tire and slipped back from the front line of defence. I was just about to get back into it after Alf yelled, 'Get the hell back up there, Tommy. They sure needs ya!' when Griller booted the ball yet again from his goal and it came out and over towards me. It came right to me. Volley. Toe. Stop and look. No one. Absolutely no one.

Their keeper, who had hardly seen, much less touched, the ball during all of the game, had left his goal. Was over towards the centre on my right. Dreaming his game away. Their backs were well away. Likely dreaming, too.

A dream for me as well. A slow-motion dream. Boot. Kick. Kick and off. Follow up. Don't give them a chance to know what's happening. Heading right for the open, wondrously open goal. Unattended goal. Head start on their keeper. Their keeper gets lost; lost in a jumbled huddle of their lot trying, trying desperately, to get back and cover.

Too late! Too late!

'Come on, Tommy . . .'

'That's my boy! That's my boy . . .'

'Go it, Tom . . .'

'You've got it . . .'

'You've got 'em . . .'

'Come on! Come on! Come on!'

Loud. Louder. Loudest.

BOOT IN. G-O-A-L!!!

The heavens seemed to open. The joy was everything.

And that, no matter how hard they tried to set things right, was that.

'Youse little beauts! Youse little beauts! Youse lotta done it at last!' Coach Alf.

Our part of the crowd erupted in a wild round of cheering as the ref blew the final whistle. The other part of the crowd didn't stay around for too long.

'Damn fluke,' said Mr Crow to Mr Harvey.

'They earned every bit of it, Jack,' said Mr Harvey.

We hugged and kissed and jumped and hugged and kissed in truly wild soccer fashion.

'Youse little beauts,' was all Alf could say.

Mrs Poppy Gibson cracked open the cask of wine Alf had told her not to get out earlier.

'They proved their point. They've proved their point,' said Mum, sounding like a lawyer. 'I just knew they would do it,' and she gave me a very un-lawyer-like hug and kiss.

Griller did a victory lap, waving Mrs Spinks' umbrella at the last few of Team A who had stuck around. Those who had stayed came up and shook hands. 'We shoulda had you, Tom,' said their captain, Andrew, the Carlos Gibson clone. 'But well done, anyway.'

'Thanks, Andy,' I said. 'We'll talk it over on Monday, eh? Reckon there's one or two things I just might be able to help you with. Right?'

Ms Hennessey kissed me, I must be truthful. She kissed everyone, even Eugene, and that sure took some doing in a vertical position.

'Well done, Tom-tit,' said Lav and she punched me lovingly on the arm. 'You're the greatest, kid.'

'I can only ever be that with your help, and with you right there beside me, Lavender,' I said, seriously.

'True,' said Lavender with all that great honesty of hers. 'Let's face it. I was up front doing all the work while you were lounging round having a rest.'

After all the hugging and kissing Mrs Lupescu whisked poor old Bog away. I just hoped that tonight was not going to be one big anti-climax for the kid, after the thrill of his morning.

We had quite a late-morning party in spite of the rain falling. 'It's God,' said Maggie. 'God is cwying tears for poor old Gweenhill A. Come on Gwiller. You can walk me home.'

Heaven and bliss. Absolute heaven and bliss. And they all looked so proud of us as they chatted and drank and ate cold sausage rolls and tried to get under three or four umbrellas.

What a morning of what a day!

Mrs Lupescu had done a big block booking for all our lot. Probably she was scared no one would turn up to see her Boggy. Surprisingly, they did.

Except for Peter and Paula and Gordon, all of whom had to go and see grandparents or other distant relatives, all our soccer team turned out to support our fellow team member, Boggy Lupescu. There were seven of us in his audience. Bog didn't need a seat because they kept him out back waiting for his turn.

Our concert crowd was much the same as our sports crowd. It never stops amazing me that the people I know and love have such wide sporting and cultural interests.

Mum and Dad, Sue and Carlos Gibson, Mr and Mrs Smith and Mr Alf Smith with Ms Hennessey. Mrs Poppy Gibson and Lavender and Eugene. Griller and Mr Spinks and yes, readers, he *was* the very little man. Dotted elsewhere in the vast audience I spotted Mr Harvey and a little old lady I took to be either his wife or his mother. Dear Miss Webster, teacher to Boggy, me and Lavender, was sitting on the other side of Mr Harvey. What a day we, her pupils, had given her! Mr and Mrs Ng Ho Hanh and about five little Ng Ho Hanhs were sitting just in front of us. Mrs Lupescu had sure done her best to fill up the place for her son. I had a very good time waving to many of the crowd when there was a gap in the music.

Apart from those of my acquaintance, there were about two thousand others. Plus the orchestra, of course, and the television crew. Lav and me tried to keep at least one of our four eyes on those cameras. No sense wasting a golden opportunity like this. Such a pity, too, that Mum, at the very last minute, would not let me wear my dinner suit. I always think one should dress well for an occasion like this. 'I think so, too,' Mum had said as she sent me to change.

Our Regional Orchestra is really very good and is often seen doing its stuff on telly. Tonight they had a guest conductor, an older guy from the northern hemisphere. This probably explains why they played a lot of northern hemisphere type music.

Boggy was the main bit in the second half, so we had to drag through an awful lot before he got to have a go. We had the very bright *Thieving Magpie* overture by an Italian called Rossini. Quite a jolly little number and easy listening, but fairly tough work for the orchestra, who have to go at it pretty quick. A lot of notes in this one.

Then it was Tchaikovsky. Not one of my best composers, Tchaikovsky. He is dead now and has been for some long time, which is probably just as well. If he was alive today I doubt if he'd make a decent living out of his music. I think he's a bit over-done or over-blown. Least this is what I've heard Mrs Lupescu say, and who am I to argue with the mother of a musical genius?

Half-time.

Then a hush of great expectancy. The moment we had all come for had arrived. Half the orchestra had taken off somewhere. I consider this a great pity and a bit lousy. You'd think they could have stayed and given a hand with one poor kid's debut, or hung around to see if he made any mistakes. It was quite likely something to do with their union demanding that the ones who play the most must have longer rests. Might even be why the Boggys of this world get to have a go in the first place.

All of us yelled and clapped as Bog was led out by the conductor. You'd have thought he could have found his own way there just by following where the noise came from. 'Right on, Bog!' and similar calls came from our row, and most of the other spectators also seemed quite pleased to see him. Boggy bowed and sat down to play the piano. He looked real good. I would have preferred to see him in a nice suit of tails and a white tie, but I guess that now, at the beginning, sort of, he couldn't afford it. He wore a pale grey suit, a white shirt, black shoes and a red tie – to show, I suppose, he was a Central European.

There are some who say that Mozart is over-rated and all he did was write a great lot of things that all sound the same and have far too many notes, a bit like Rossini's *Magpie* has. Well, I'm not one of them. I think Mozart was a genius, as quite a few people say, and that Boggy looks like a suitable sort of person to fit in his shoes.

In my humble opinion Boggy played his Mozart better than Mozart probably did himself.

Not perfect, mind you. But let's face it, Bog is still a kid. I thought he took the first movement a bit slow. Mind you, it is the slow movement, but there's no sense dragging out the agony, as they say. Also he couldn't be seen to race too far ahead of what was left of the orchestra.

A great sigh rose from the crowd as he came to the last of it. Either they were pleased it was at last over, or else they were happy he had remembered all the notes.

Then he had a wee rest while the audience had a cough and a couple of violins had a tune-up. Then, with a friendly nod to his conductor, he was back at it again. He had sure needed his rest because the next bit is lightning fast. Note after note after note. Could never make out why this part never worried Bog much. I knew it back to front and up and down because he played it so much. To show off, I always reckoned. It had always been the third movement that really got him. Surprising, because it's another drag-it-out slow bit.

He finished the fast part and his orchestra came in a close second. They nearly made it together. Quite a few of the spectators gave him a good clap. As us concert-goers know, this is not really on, and I frowned meaningfully at Griller, Maggie and Brian. You're supposed to wait till the end and it's all over before you let loose with a good clap. Rather stupid idea, really. What if part one is good and parts two and three are the pits? End up getting next to nothing for at least a bit of good work.

The third movement was a deeply moving experience for Lavender and me, and we held hands. How often had we listened to our good friend, Bog, explain his personal agony over getting into the soul of this bit, and whether he'd ever get the damn thing right? This time he sure did, and just having him get quietly and carefully through it without a mistake was enough to bring a tear to my old eye. To my mind and ear, I doubt that he even missed one note. What was left of the orchestra did their bit, too.

The crowd went wild. We were the wildest of all. Mrs Poppy Gibson crying her eyes out and yelling, 'Bravo! Bravo! Bravo!' and soon all of us joined in with her. Everyone was standing in order to stretch their legs after such a long piece, and still clapping.

Bog bowed and took off. He came back. Bowed and took off again. Six times. Would've saved a helluva lot of time if he'd just stayed put. The telly cameras followed his every movement and I'm positive they hit on us down in the front.

On his sixth trip back some woman gave him a bunch of flowers. A strange present, I thought, for someone like Bog. I knew he would've preferred a soccer ball. Still, Mrs Lupescu might like some of them.

Bogdan Lupescu: world famous piano player and adolescent prodigy.

As I say, what a day! What a night!

Dad told me next day that the party at our place lasted till it was light next morning. Not that I remember much about it. Us younger adults, or so I'm told, didn't last for even an hour of fun and frolic. The pace of life had caught up with us, and we snored off wherever we could find a bed or comfy corner.

CHAPTER TWELVE A

IN WHICH IT IS WISER NOT TO CALL IT CHAPTER 13

'I am of the opinion you'll soon need a manager, agent and publicity person, Boggy,' I said to him as he, Lavender and I sat, Sunday evening, warming our chill bones in the last rays of a dead-loss winter sun on the steps of the branch library.

'You reckon?' said Bog.

'I do, indeed. You don't want to be letting too many golden opportunities slip by you. What with all the practising you'll have to do, you won't have the time to do the organising yourself. You'll need a minder, mark my words.' And who better than a close friend? I was thinking. If last night's crowd was anything to go by there'd sure be more than a few golden opportunities.

'There won't be much playing for the next five years. Dad says I gotta finish ordinary school.'

'What a waste,' said Lavender. 'Strike while the iron's hot, I'd say. Better watch your fingers don't dry up on you.'

'That's one thing about soccer,' I said. 'You can do soccer and school at the same time.'

Winter's sun flickered its last and we stood to go. 'What next?' asked Lav.

'We go home,' I said, simply.

'No, dummo,' she said, nicely. 'Where to from here?'

I have noticed that sometimes she has these sort of mental blockages. 'We go down North Street, Lav, and through the traffic lights. Remember? Then through the Square and turn first right. Don't worry, Lav. It's easy. Just follow me.' True, quite true. She would always be able to count on me.

'Lavender means after soccer. What do we do after soccer?' said Boggy.

'Thank you, Boggy,' said Lavender.

'After soccer there's soccer,' I said. 'We still got three games.'

'I know that,' said Lav. 'I also know that not one of us except old Griller, and that sure is funny, is even a soccer player's bum. Get me?'

It was hard not to. 'I dunno,' I said.

'I do,' said Boggy. 'Face it, Tom. Lavender is right, in a way. We've done it, eh? We proved our point and we had a lot of fun.'

'And a lot of hard work,' said Lavender. 'But I know I'll never be a woman soccer player of great fame, no matter how much I write about it. Plumbing's more my line.'

'And if any of us want to play in a team next season, I reckon old Crow would be forced to give us a decent chance,' said Boggy.

Was my house of cards tumbling about my ears? Was I hearing right?

'Besides,' said Lav, 'one or two other things I want to have a go at, and I can't fit them all in and keep everything going at home, what with Poppy and Eugene and Carlos still smoking.'

132

'Cricket?' I asked. Not quite the right time of year to be thinking of cricket unless you happen to live in the northern hemisphere country of England, which has summer like our winter and at just about the same time.

'Don't think so,' said Bog. 'Don't reckon Mum'd let me, even with gloves.'

'You going to insure your hands, Boggy?' asked Lavender.

'What d'you mean, insure?' asked Bog, who isn't too good at the maths side of things.

'Tennis?' I asked.

'Nah,' said Lav. 'And don't mention synchronised swimming again. We done that. Remember?'

'Well,' I said, more brightly than I felt, 'I guess we'll come up with something.'

The sun set, and a light seemed to go out of my life along with it.

The light came back on the next day on the stage with the other captains.

'. . . in what has truly been described as one of the more memorable sporting victories ever given to a Greenhill Intermediate team . . .'

'John,' said Mr Harvey. 'Your brief, five-sentence report on your match is already in danger of lasting as long as the actual match, which, I might add, many of us saw. A great credit to your team and your persistence. Now, lad, get to the point.'

Everything had built up to this moment, and it should have been much more than just saying, 'Greenhill Intermediate Soccer Team C defeated Greenhill Intermediate Team A 1–0', which is what I did.

They do say that climbing a mountain actually means more than standing on the top. I think I know what they mean. But, ah, no one, no one at all, can rob us of that magic, magic moment when we did actually stand there. Not ever.

Afterwards? Well, life ticks merrily on, as they say. We played our other three games. Drew one of them, 1–1. Lost the others 2–1 and 3–1. We ended up second to bottom on the competition table, but as dear Alf says, 'Winning isn't everything but it sure beats pickin' yer nose.'

Another magical moment in my life so far was going up to receive the Precision Tool & Die Ltd Cup for Most Improved Junior Soccer Team from the graceful and important hands of Councillor Phyllis Black, chairperson of the City Council Recreation and Cultural Amenities Committee, and patroness of the Soccer Association; a charming older person who may frequently be seen shopping at the Poppy G. Boutique and Accessory Bar, and is one of my Dad's employers and bosses.

Then it was hang up the old boots time, so to speak. They weren't that old. Dad said they cost a bomb back in May when he bought them for me. Light years ago in time and space. Mum said to be sure and clean the boots before I hung them up.

Alf collected the shirts. I felt sure he needed to hide them from the prying eyes of the law. It wasn't until very much later and in idle conversation during a lull in a further exciting episode of my life and times, that dear Ms Smith, the former Ms Hennessey that was, true friend that she's become, told me they had never fallen off the back of a truck at all. 'Stupid little goose, it was a figure of speech. Alf bought them out of his own pocket. Just shows how much he did for youse all. Anyway, Tommy, even if he had, I'm sure your Mum wouldn't have charged too much to defend him.' Which meant I had to go to the long trouble of explaining the difference between commercial and criminal law.

And what, you may well ask, of the others who have peopled the pages of this rich tale? What, indeed.

Griller Spinks, as I write this, is very big in cricket, and a star sportsperson. An enormous batting ability, and no one's got a hope of hitting a wicket with Grill standing in front of it. It's not too clever to hit him, either, if he's holding a bat. My mate Grill. Now that life has opened up its gates and rewards to him he's given up hanging and smoking. Very friendly with Maggie Smith. As she says in that cute way of hers, 'Gwiller gives me a weal buzz.' I'm not surprised.

Mrs Poppy Gibson and Eugene are still, as they say, a number. 'He's too much of a good thing for me to ever let go,' she often says. I suppose if you're lucky enough to get a grip on two metres of man you'd be a fool to let go. She says she plans a late autumn wedding and I heard Dad say to Mum, 'Well, it fits with her time of life.'

Mum said, 'Florrie'll grow up one day,' and sometime later added, 'but not too soon I hope.'

Carlos Gibson? I don't know. I suppose, underneath it all, I have a soft spot for Carlos for all he is brutal to man and beast, and often to me, and for all that he smokes. He'll learn his lesson there one day. Smoking truly ages a person, inside and out. Wrinkled baggy skin, runny eyes and rotted lungs. No sign of it happening to superhunk Carlos Gibson yet, more's the pity, and I've sure looked real close. In true, kindly and almost-brother-in-law fashion, I've even offered to go and buy his cigarettes for him.

Boggy is away for two months with Mr and Mrs Lupescu in Central Europe. They've taken a video with them of The Concert, and they're sort of flogging Boggy around at the same time as Mr Lupescu is stocking up on railway engines, shotguns and caviar for another round of selling in the southern hemisphere. They're catching up on their friends and relatives, too. I think we all know what that means.

Mum, Dad and Sue are all okay. I know Carlos Gibson is not a good man, but the love of him does have a soothing effect on my sister.

Mr Harvey? Kindly as ever, always ready to offer an interested ear. As soccer wound down I took to calling on him more often and he seemed to enjoy our little chats. He was, indeed, the reason for me writing all this.

'It's always nice to have you in here, Don,' he said, 'and I'm always willing to hear, yet again, how you managed the whole thing, and the major part you have played in reforming Dwayne Spinks. I have a feeling your future could well lie in social work, lad. But I do have a suggestion.'

'Yes, Mr Harvey?' How perceptive he was. Clearly one of those who had not got where they got just by having a pretty face.

'Why don't you go away for, oh, some long time and write it all down? I have a gut feeling it would make a far better story than the private life of the amoeba.'

Who am I to ignore the advice of an older and wiser man? So, I did.

At the very end of the day there is always Lavender. I reckon there always will be. Well, in all truth, if not Lavender then someone else not unlike her. If such a person exists.

It is well that our interests are the same, and there is so much give and take between us. It does sometimes seem, however, that I do all the giving and she does all the taking – and when she says, 'Presbyterian Ladies, Thursday at four,' I'm expected to jump. It may well be a problem with your run-of-the-mill feminist woman; the boot's always on the other foot. I have mentioned this problem to Dad. All he says is that in these matters I have had far greater experience than him. He also says he's never met a radical feminist woman and, if you ask him, Lavender is nothing more than a chip off that old block, Mrs Poppy Gibson, her mother. It was a great comfort when he told me that in his opinion, not only did I have the right equipment, but also the right attitude, and that Lav's brief fling with Alf was no more than the age-old attraction your younger woman has for your older man. Dad should know.

'I've got it,' says Lav.

'Well, get rid of it before it stings,' I say.

'Shut up, dummo, and listen. Look. We've done for soccer, right?'

I might have put it in a different way. 'If you say so, Lav.'

'We've had a gutful of being competitive and competing and all that?'

'If you say so, Lav.'

'We're going to take over culture next,' she says.

'Whose culture?' I ask.

'Culture with a capital D,' says Lav.

'Explain,' I sigh.

'Ms Hennessey, I mean the new Ms Smith, has coughed at the wrong time again,' says Lavender.

'What d'you mean?'

'I mean Mr Harvey says what a wonderful job she did with us in soccer. She's doing drama next. The school play. The big D.'

'Is that the name of it?'

'All that time you spend with Grill has cooked your brain,' says Lavender. 'I think she intends doing a new production of *Snow White*.'

'With Grill and you as the dwarfs?' I ask.

She ignores me. 'I fully intend auditioning for the leading role.'

'Snow White?'

'I'm more interested in what can be done with the part of the Wicked Queen,' she says.

'Yeah. Reckon that would suit you better,' I say.

'What d'you mean?' she asks sharply.

'Well, it's something to get your teeth into,' I say. 'Snow White, if you ask me, is a bit of a wimp. She's sure no radical feminist.'

'You're quite right, Tom-tit. The Queen actually is your classical radical feminist. I've had a chat with Ms Hennessey-Smith. I've told her that you, me, Boggy when he gets back, even poor Maggie – in truth, Tommy, most of our soccer team – could sure beat the knickers off anyone else wanting a part in her play.'

'Reckon you're right, Lav,' I say. 'Did I ever tell you what that fur coat does for you?' Maybe she was right about the big D. It was time for a change. As I've always said, your well-rounded man needs a well-rounded woman and they both need well-rounded interests.

A USEFUL GUIDE TO THE VERY MANY READERS OF THIS BOOK

The following words, in true alphabet order, are those I may have used that need a bit more explanation:

boutique	A trendy clothes shop where you pay a bundle and a bomb for the same clothes you get one year later at the Presbyterian Ladies.
child prodigy	A kid, male or female, who is as good or better at something than an outstanding adult, e.g. Bogdan Lupescu, a child prodigy of a piano player.
Count Dracula	A Central European spook. Drinks blood. Never dies. Star of many a Hollywood film.
Diego Maradona	A star soccer player from Argentina, a country in the depths of South America, e.g. *Don't Cry for me, Argentina*, a well-known and popular older song. Not known whether sung by D. Maradona.

Ms	The title used by those women who do not choose to Miss or Mrs themselves, e.g. Ms Hennessey. You can't tell whether she's married or not, but it doesn't matter these days to thinking people.
northern hemisphere	The top half of the world that we of the south don't inhabit, e.g. Portugal and Central Europe and the remains of Pope Pius X and Mozart are all in the northern hemisphere, as is Pocatello, Idaho. Argentina is not.
Pocatello, Idaho	A North American centre in the good old US of A.
Pope Pius X	An ageing Roman Catholic leader, now dead. Often referred to as a saint. He'd sure need to be if he's got anything to do with the school of the same name in our suburb.
Portuguese	Portugal is a country and Portuguese live in it, e.g. Carlos Gibson may be Portuguese but he sure doesn't live there. Worse luck!
Presbyterian Ladies	Second-hand clothes dealers and pretty good at it, too.
Wolfgang A. Mozart	A somewhat famous composer (music writer) of about two hundred years ago. Very bright, e.g. probably a baby prodigy rather than a child prodigy.

Lived one helluva life and died broke. Buried in a common hole somewhere in Central Europe, e.g. I've seen the film. Whew! Some guy.

Tchaikovsky Salvation Army rugby league muesli Rossini anorexia slam-dunk etcetera etcetera

It doesn't bother me if you don't know these. If you can't read them, miss them out and it won't make much difference. If you want to know, well, look them up yourself.

ABOUT THE AUTHOR

William Taylor was born in Lower Hutt, New Zealand, and now lives in Ohakune, on the south-western slopes of Mt Ruapehu. A school teacher for many years, he began writing in 1970. His first book for older children, *Pack Up, Pick Up and Off*, first published in 1981, enjoyed considerable success. His more recent titles include *My Summer of the Lions* and *Shooting Through*, both published in Puffin in 1988. He was awarded the Choysa Bursary for Children's Writers in 1985. William Taylor now devotes himself full time to writing. His interests include gardening, reading and music. He has two sons.

ALL WE KNOW
Simon French

Arkie Gerhardt lives in Sydney. She's twelve years old and she's thinking a lot these days — about Mum and Michael and Jo, and Ian from down the road who's become part of the family. About Kylie who used to be her best friend, and her favourite teacher, Mr Clifton, who's going away. She's taking lots of photographs too with the camera Michael gave her because that's a way of holding on to the things you know when so much is changing.

A perceptive novel about growing up from the author of *Hey Phantom Singlet* and *Cannily, Cannily*.

All We Know was voted Book of the Year for older readers by the Children's Book Council of Australia in 1987.

THE TRUE STORY OF
SPIT MACPHEE
James Aldridge

The people of St Helen are concerned for young Spit MacPhee. Spit lives a hand to mouth existence with his eccentric grandfather, Fyfe MacPhee, in an old shanty on the banks of the Murray River.

When old Fyfe dies the townspeople seize the opportunity to do something about vagabond Spit. He finds himself the subject of a dramatic court case which polarises the religious and moral attitudes of a typical Australian country town in the 1930s. Yet such is the strength of young Spit's character that, when the truth about his life with his grandfather is revealed, no one is left unchanged.

'A marvellous yarn, a highly enjoyable page turner, hard to put down . . .'
Walter McVitty, *Australian*